Lee's heart stood still as she recognized him

Every instinct told her to run. But there was no way to escape without looking totally undignified.

Dreading that he would realize who she was at close quarters, she watched his approach. But he was smiling lazily down at her, seeing only a woman he wanted to meet, instead of the girl he had hated so much eight years before.

He said softly, "Are you as enamored with this party as you look?" Amusement laced a deep rich voice that set her nerves tingling. "Because if you are, you're in good company." A Canadian accent—resonant, subtle. "And as we're clearly in the minority here—" wryly he directed a glance to Vince and his companions moving sinuously to the pulsing music "—I think we should stick together, don't you?"

ELIZABETH POWER was once a legal secretary, but when the compulsion to write became too strong, she abandoned affidavits, wills and conveyances in favor of a literary career. Her husband, she says, is her best critic. And he's a good cook, too—often readily taking over the preparation of meals when her writing is in full flow. They live in a three-hundred-year-old English country estate cottage, surrounded by woodlands and wildlife. Who wouldn't be inspired to write?

Books by Elizabeth Power

HARLEQUIN PRESENTS
1078—SHADOW IN THE SUN

HARLEQUIN ROMANCE
2825—RUDE AWAKENING

CHAPTER ONE

IT REALLY wasn't her scene at all.

Gazing across the stuffy, smoke-filled room at the little cliques of well-dressed men and women, the more enthusiastic throwing themselves into some lively reggae beat, Lee Roman sighed. A working holiday in Bermuda had sounded great in the confines of her New York editorial office, but what she hadn't reckoned on were parties like these, that Vince somehow always managed to dredge up.

She turned away from the spectacle in a soft whisper of creamy silk, hair falling like a dark shadow over one bare shoulder.

'Hey, Lee! Stop looking like you've lost the world in the bottom of that Martini glass, and come and join in the fun.' With a sinking feeling, she heard the photographer's exuberant Cockney tones behind her. 'You might be chief pip of *Eve's Apple*, but you're not meeting this chap Mason until tomorrow, and the magazine's hardly likely to go down the drain if the boss lets her hair down for one night.'

No, but a sense of responsibility wasn't easy to shrug off, she thought wryly—a thing her father had instilled in her from the very beginning. And it was as well that he had, she'd realised gratefully over the years, because when he had died, leaving her, a frightened adolescent alone in a strange country, she had needed every ounce of that initiative and integrity to survive.

It was all right for Vince, she thought, glancing from his fair, rather boyish features to the leggy blonde who

5

clung adoringly to his arm. He might have had time to find new diversions since their plane had touched down that day, but she couldn't be as carefree. She and Vince Harris might be the same age, but at twenty-five she was having to cope with worrying problems like the sliding sales of her magazine, along with awkward industrialists who wouldn't wholly commit themselves to being interviewed, as well as refusing to see anyone from the *Apple* in a less senior position than herself.

'Just think yourself lucky no definite time's been arranged for the photo-sessions with Mason, otherwise you could well have found yourself flying out on one plane and back home on the next,' she said. 'Make sure you're around when I need you,' she went on to advise with a modicum of authority, though a smile was softening her rather angular features, adding warmth to the aquamarine eyes, because she liked Vince. Mutual English roots had sparked an instant rapport between them as soon as she'd taken him on to her team two years ago, apart from the fact that he was the best photographer she had. 'And contrary to your well-meaning advice. . .' she glanced down at the wide-brimmed glass in her hand '. . .as soon as I've finished this drink I'm going back to the hotel.'

The music had changed to a slow, sensuous rock, causing a restlessness in the other girl, who—Lee couldn't help deducing wryly—looked as if she'd given the adjective to the phrase 'dumb blonde'. Impatiently, she was pulling at the man's arm.

'OK, sweetheart.' He shrugged beneath the light jacket, and shot Lee a covertly triumphant grin. 'You ought to stick around, too,' he was recommending somewhat tentatively, low enough so that his young companion couldn't hear. 'I know work comes first, and men tend to take a back seat in your life, but it

would do you good to get yourself wholly involved with
someone for once. . .like the guy who hasn't been able
to take his eyes off you for the past half-hour.'

Lee tensed, oddly embarrassed. So Vince had
noticed him, too. From out of the corner of her eye
she had been uncomfortably aware that someone had
been watching her for some time, and from across the
arching, reddish bracts of a huge shrimp plant she sent
a surreptitious glance to the dark-haired man standing
by the bar.

He was tall—probably the tallest man here tonight,
she would have said—and superbly built, too, the lines
of that physique beneath the dark lounge-suit marking
him a man who believed in keeping himself in the peak
of condition. Then he glanced up, swiftly and unexpectedly, almost as if he had felt her silent appraisal
across the crowded room, and dark, penetrating eyes
locked with hers. And suddenly she found herself
breaking out into a cold sweat, tearing her gaze away
with a small gasp of startling recognition. *No! No. It
couldn't be.*

'Wow! What a dish! If a man like that showed any
interest in me, I'd go all funny and wouldn't know what
to say.'

Dazedly, Lee heard the blonde's inane comment,
then Vince's sarcastic 'Thanks!' before he hustled the
girl away. Stealing another glance up, Lee was horrified
to realise that not only had the man left the bar, but
that, unbelievably, he was coming over!

Every instinct told her to run. Only the inability to
escape without looking totally undignified prevented
her from doing so. Even so, she watched his approach
with reluctant awareness of that elegance he still possessed, of the female attention he attracted with that

authoritative, dark presence, the high, intellectual forehead, that proud nose and the determination in that thrusting jaw, lending him a sophistication that set him apart from every other man in the room.

Dreading he would notice her alarm—realise who she was at close quarters—Lee's heart seemed to stand still. But he was smiling lazily down at her, seeing only a woman he wanted to meet, instead of the girl he had hated with such vehemence eight years before, as he said softly, 'Are you as enamoured with this party as you look?' Amusement laced a deep, rich voice that set her nerves jangling, the brown eyes, fringed by long lashes, gazing cordially down into hers. 'Because if you are, you're in good company.' A Canadian accent, of course. Resonant. Subtle. 'And as we're clearly in the minority here. . .' wryly, he directed a glance to where Vince and his companion were moving sinuously to the pulsing music '. . . I think we should stick together, don't you?' That gaze, moving over her fine-boned features, momentarily robbed her of speech. She caught her breath as those black brows knitted, as he studied the feathered layers of her long, dark hair, the slightly upturned nose and the mouth she considered too wide, and her heart thudded in her breast. Would he remember her?

Almost breathlessly, he asked, 'What's your name?'

So he hadn't! Relief was enervating, and she leaned back against the wall behind her, needing its support. But of course he wouldn't, she tried reassuring herself. She might have recognised him, but he had merely matured, while she had flowered from gawky adolescence into womanhood. She even had a different name.

'Lee.'

A muscle moved at the corner of his mouth—a cruel, sensuous mouth that all those years ago had been twisted in bitter hatred for her, yet which now appeared faintly amused. And gently, so persuasively that she had a job convincing herself this *was* the same man, he pressed, 'Lee what?'

A little voice inside her urged her to tell him to go to hell. That, after the way he had treated her before, the only sensible thing to do was to get away from him—and fast! But she seemed to have tossed off her common sense with her fourth Martini, and against all rational judgement she was uttering coolly, 'Just Lee.'

His gaze, falling to her lips, flooded her cheeks with colour, that line between the dark eyes making her suddenly afraid that her voice, at least, might have struck some chord of familiarity with him, though she knew the years in New York had all but erased the obvious English accent she had once had. But he was saying casually enough, 'Just implies "mere"—"insignificance"—and I wouldn't have said there was anything mere or insignificant about you, Lee.' With any other man she might have laughed aside the compliment as trite flattery, but he wasn't any other man, and she was annoyed when her pulse throbbed unexpectedly in response. He was dismissing her reluctance to convey anything further about herself, though, by adding on a more level note, 'Mine's Colyer. Jordan Colyer.' As if she needed telling! 'Can I get you another drink?' If she winced at the name, then he didn't see it, for he was glancing down at the glass she was still holding.

'I think I've had quite enough already, thanks.' She smiled away his offer with mock sincerity, drained her glass, and looked around for somewhere to put it. She flinched as he took it from her, the casual contact of his hand impinging, leaving her struggling for composure as he gave the glass to a passing waiter who had seemed to materialise, as if by magic, for him.

'Tell me, Lee. . .is it equally imprudent to ask what you're doing here?'

Obviously the withholding of her name had piqued him, and beneath the warm intensity of his gaze her mouth formed a small curve of bitter satisfaction. Oh, to get to him! Hurt him as he'd hurt her eight years ago, when he'd so wrongly accused her of being a harlot and a gold-digger! But, above the heavy beat of the music, she said calmly, 'Where?' One fine eyebrow lifted. 'At this party? Or in Bermuda?'

'Both. But let's start with Bermuda.' He sounded as if he was losing patience with her, she thought, pleased, realising that this was one conquest he wasn't finding as easy as he'd obviously anticipated. She had no doubt that usually he wouldn't have to try very hard.

A cacophony of laughter and clapping had him glancing over his shoulder to where Vince and the blonde were impressing onlookers with a finale of contortions that had eyes bulging.

'Is he your boyfriend?' A swift, downward glance had shown him that she was wearing no rings.

Lee shook her head.

'Well, it's obvious he isn't a blood relative,' he remarked decisively, eyes tugging over her dark, delicate features. 'Therefore I can only deduce that you must be bound together by business.'

How very astute of him! She looked up at him, reluctantly impressed, an unwelcome *frisson* shooting through her as her eyes met the dark penetration of his.

He was older, of course, than she remembered him, though he'd gained no excess weight over the years. He looked as fit and lean as he ever had, that raw magnetism about him more compelling in its maturity, that underlying sexuality she'd only been half aware of before striking her now with such flagrant potency that she realised her fingers were twining agitatedly in the soft fabric of her dress. She knew she would have been wise to have left there and then, but an alcohol-induced rashness was prompting her to ask, 'What about you? Is there a Mrs Colyer somewhere around?' Eight years ago there hadn't been. But eight years was a long time.

'Neither maternal, nor nuptial,' he surprised her by answering then, and with such a disarming smile that her heart skipped a beat. Any other woman would have been utterly smitten, she thought, resenting that powerful male aura he possessed. Someone passed them with a tray of drinks, forcing him closer to her, sharpening her senses to the tantalising spice of some cologne he had used. 'I'm thirty-five. I lived in New York. And I'm here tonight because protocol demanded it,' he was saying, as though he thought she expected a full dossier on him, 'although my business enterprises are rather too varied—and boring. . .' this with a sideways tug of his mouth '. . .to list at this moment. Apart from the fact that I'd rather hear about yours.'

I'll bet you would! She flashed him a smile that didn't touch her eyes, having no intention of telling him anything about herself, or that the interviews she was hoping to secure with Alec Mason could well be a swan-song or a lifeline for *Eve's Apple*. The backsliding of a magazine which she had financed and built up over the years was too delicate a subject to share with anyone who wasn't directly involved—least of all Jordan Colyer. And she knew all about *his* enterprises anyway. Even at twenty-seven he'd been king of his own business empire, and with a hard-headed brain like his he had to be worth millions now. She also knew she should have run a mile the instant she'd seen him coming. But she hadn't. And now she was witnessing another side to the man, which held a dangerous fascination for her—that of the predatory male animal who had seen the chance of a likely mate, and was using all the sway of that powerful magnetism to try and lure her into his bed.

Sending him a coquettish smile that shocked even herself, she murmured, 'Let's just leave it that it's business, mmm?'

Her reticence was acknowledged in the darkening of his eyes, in the hard pull of his mouth, but soft mockery played around his lips as he regarded the pure fragility of her features.

'You're very beautiful,' he said huskily, moving in to rest his hand on the wall just above her shoulder, so that she had the sudden, disconcerting feeling of being trapped. 'You're also very, very secretive.'

And you, she thought acridly—feeling his warm, whisky-tinged breath against her cheek—are very, very charming. So much so that she had to force herself to remember how brutal he could be. Oh, not physically, she recalled bitterly, her lips tightening, because he hadn't laid a finger on her all those years ago. He hadn't needed to stoop to such undignified lengths to demoralise her—hurt her. Just his cruel accusations when he'd called her the lowest form of her sex had seen to that. She shuddered, remembering. Ironic, she thought, that now *she* should have the advantage over *him*. And suddenly a reckless idea occurred to her. If he was flattering himself that he had found a likely catch in her, then let him think it! Looking up into the hard structure of his face, she knew a little tremor of nerves, but managed a demure smile in spite of it. 'I'm also suffocating from the heat in this place.' She fanned a cooling hand before her face, looking across the smoky room to the bar and the steps that led up to the terrace with a deliberately wistful sigh. 'Do you think you could get me out of here?'

He acquiesced with the barest tilt of his head, the hand at her elbow evoking another small ripple of nerves as he began guiding her between the tables and small groups of people. Seeing Vince looking at her interestedly from the dance area added strength to her plans, and momentarily she excused herself, while berating herself for a sudden bout of misgivings. What she was planning would be no more than Jordan deserved, she thought grievously, the memory of his flaying hatred still able to make her recoil inside as she came up to a rather smug-looking Vince.

'All right. . .so I've taken your advice about that silent admirer,' she bluffed, before he could say anything, while the blonde was staring agog at the tall man standing a few yards away from them as if Lee had just landed the prize catch of Bermuda. 'I'm going out on to the terrace, but I want you to come up. . .' she dropped a glance at her slim silver wristwatch '. . .at exactly eleven o'clock to offer to take me home.'

'Gosh! My luck's really in tonight, baby.' He grinned at the younger girl, but Lee wasn't in the mood for his usual flippancy.

'Vince, I'm deadly serious,' she emphasised as the band struck up into a rendition of a slow ballad. 'And if you want to continue enjoying these exotic locations at the expense of *Eve's Apple*, you'd better do as I ask.' She didn't like resorting to blackmail, but she was desperate that he shouldn't let her down, and sometimes, with Vince, it was the only way. 'Just be there—that's all I'm asking,' she hissed, careful that Jordan didn't hear her. 'Promise me you'll do it?'

It was more of a plea than a warning, so that Vince responded with, 'OK, OK, I'll be there.'

She had butterflies in her stomach as she allowed Jordan to lead her up the steps and past the lifts, although her nerves were soothed a little as they stepped out into the cool darkness of the terrace, the view taking her breath away.

They were overlooking Hamilton Harbour, the lights from the buildings on the other side twinkling at them across the water, though they paled against the tiers of fairylike stars illuminating the cruise ships in the fore-ground, splendid floating hotels, dispatching their tour-ists to the restaurants and nightclubs of the capital.

'Your first time in Bermuda?'

She shrugged. 'Is it that obvious?'

He nodded, his eyes glimmering with soft laughter, and something else. Desire, she thought, with a sudden tightening of her throat, and looked away to the couples dancing to the soft music that drifted out from the hotel, figures silhouetted by the concealed lighting in the shrubbery. The perfume of some exotic plant wafted towards her, gentle and evocative on the tangy sea breeze.

'Would you care for this one, Lee?'

Pulse accelerating, she stiffened, but went into his arms, knowing a refusal wouldn't help her plans at all. She had to be nice to him, regardless of how sickening the thought was, she told herself, although she couldn't help flinching as his arms went around her, the fear that he might suddenly realise her identity stretching her nerves as tight as a bowstring.

'Relax.' Above the music, his voice was soft and persuasive. 'Are you usually so tense when a man asks you to dance?'

Of course. He could tell.

She swallowed, wondering for one brief moment if she were wise going ahead with what she was intending, but a nagging little voice inside her told her that she owed it to herself. So, with her lips upturned, just inches from that forceful jaw, she purred, 'It depends on the man,' controlling the situation in spite of herself—in spite of the sudden, disturbing contact of that hard body so close to hers.

She heard him laugh softly. 'Do I take that as a compliment, Lee?'

His proximity and the spicy scent of him was disorientating, making her breathing quicken, her mouth dry, and her lips trembled as she smiled up at him to say sweetly, 'Why not? You will anyway.'

He laughed again, more loudly this time, the sound deep and vibrant on the night air. 'You know, Miss Whoever-you-are, for someone so lovely, you're surprisingly blunt.'

But not as blunt as she was going to be, she thought, with a small shiver.

She touched her tongue to her lips, her fingers sliding provocatively beneath his jacket, making her startlingly aware of the stirring warmth of him—of the solid muscle beneath the fine shirt. 'I thought you said I was secretive?' She couldn't believe she was acting this way with him—a man who hated her, she reminded herself chasteningly, although she knew she had to if her plan was to succeed.

'You're obviously a woman of extremes.' His features were crossed with dark shadows as he smiled down at her, his voice as warm and seductive as the music. 'Which means that probably behind that cool façade of yours lurks a very passionate nature.'

A ship's horn sounded somewhere out in the harbour, and unaccountably Lee shivered. How wrong he

was, she thought. She'd never yet met a man who had
interested her enough to warrant such complete abandon of the senses. But, in her most beguiling tone, she
breathed, 'And you're obviously burning with curiosity
to find out. Well, just to satisfy *my* curiosity,
Jordan. . .' she slipped her arms enticingly around his
neck, the open invitation of her smile hiding the self-
recrimination she was battling with inside '. . .do you
do *everything* as well as you dance?'

One black eyebrow lifted, and she gave a small gasp
as his arm suddenly tightened around her, every cell
awakening to the totally unnerving maleness of him.

'There's no comparison,' he murmured drily, his
voice caressing her. 'Compared with some things I do,
my dancing only qualifies for the amateur.'

The utter conceit of the man! It took all her will-
power not to pull forcibly away from him, let him know
exactly what she thought of him and his conceit. But it
wasn't time yet. She had to wait for Vince. When she
had the other man's moral support, she would take
immense satisfaction in ditching him!

'Really?' she murmured huskily, angling her slender
body tantalisingly closer to his, self-censure clogging
every pore. Nevertheless, she forced her gaze to drop
wantonly to his lips, and uttered, 'Perhaps we should
work on a few new steps together.'

She heard him catch a breath. 'Are you as friendly
with everyone?' he enquired, amusement—but something that might have been disapproval, too—tugging
at his mouth. 'Or is it just my riveting personality that
you find so difficult to resist?'

She was acting like a first-rate whore, and he knew
it, she thought with raging shame, but she couldn't
back down now, and answered with a smile, in a voice
laced with innuendo, 'I'll leave that for you to decide.'

She felt him tense, saw the dark query in his eyes, and she had to fight to control an inner trembling, aware that he was more masculine than any other man she had met in her life.

'Where are you staying, Lee? Here?'

So he was getting around to it. Shaping his questions for the one reason he had walked across to her tonight—to satisfy the irrepressible urge to mate.

She shook her head, trying not to look as if there were a nervous tightening in her stomach, deciding she wouldn't be giving too much away by responding, 'On the South Shore.' A stealthy glance at her watch made her catch her breath. It was already five past eleven. Where was Vince? He should have been here by now.

'Don't pull away from me.' Her throat constricted as Jordan's arm locked like a steel bar against her back. 'Do you really think I'm letting you escape now that I've found you?'

Oh, goodness! Where was Vince? She forced herself to smile, sudden alien sensations shivering down her spine as those cool fingers played with insidious expertise across her bare back.

Ten past! She darted a panicky look towards the terrace doors, but there was no sign of the photographer and, alarmed, she realised that the other couples had been gradually drifting away, because she was entirely alone out here with Jordan now.

Quarter past! Oh, good grief! Why didn't Vince come? Surely he wouldn't let her down?

She felt herself grow hot, her palms sticky, as Jordan dipped his head, lips brushing the sensitive skin behind her earlobe, the simple action sending such an unexpected shock of pleasure tingling through her that she caught her breath, gave an involuntary little gasp. Encouraged by her response he repeated the action, his hands moving across her cool flesh, so warm and hard and stimulating. The feathering kiss, and the clean spicy scent of him, were suddenly so dangerously erotic that somehow she was tugging herself away from him, burning with shame. If Vince wasn't coming, then this had gone too far!

'What is it?' Jordan's voice was husky with desire, and even in the shadows she could see the flush of arousal under the tanned skin.

'I—I've got an early appointment tomorrow,' she uttered quickly, her thoughts in chaos, wondering how she could have so little resistance to the charms of a man she totally despised—who would still despise *her* if he knew! She darted another glance at her watch. Blast Vince! 'It's late. I—I should be going.'

'So soon?' He reached for her again, chuckling softly. 'All right. Let's get you home.'

'No!' That was the last thing she wanted—to let him know where she was staying. 'I mean. . .that isn't necessary. . .'

'Oh?' A line deepened between his eyes. 'You have your own transport?' His scepticism told her that he knew as well as she did that there were no self-drive cars available for tourists on the island.

'No, but——'

'Then I'll drive you.'

So he had his own car, Lee mused, realising through a burst of more lively music that she didn't have the faintest idea what he was doing in Bermuda; that she'd been too bent on her own revenge even to care.

Raucous singing met them as they came back into the hotel, along with the clink of glasses and noisy conversation drifting up from the ballroom. Shuddering, Lee wondered what she was going to do. The cold shoulder she had been planning for Jordan wouldn't only be less effective now, without an audience, but totally unwise, because she knew what his anger was like and it wasn't something she relished rousing while she was alone with him. Yet she didn't want him taking her back to her hotel!

'Look. . .it's kind of you. . .but it really isn't necessary,' she persisted as politely as her nerves would allow when Jordan pressed the button for one of the lifts. 'It's been nice, but I really don't think. . .well. . . that you and I——'

She broke off as he impaled her with such a censuring look that her stomach muscles tightened as though in a vice. 'What are you trying to say, Lee? Thanks, but no, thanks?' He pushed back his jacket, the hard, lean strength of him which that movement exposed causing her to lick her lips nervously, oblivious to the noise going on behind them. 'A bit of a change of heart from outside, isn't it? If my knowledge of your sex hasn't deserted me altogether, I would have said you were virtually begging me to take you to bed out there.'

'That's your interpretation. Heavens, it was only an innocent dance!' Though she managed to sound shocked, inside she was recoiling at her outrageous behaviour, and she felt her cheeks reddening, realising that she had stepped into a quagmire of her own making.

'Is that what you'd call it?' His tone was harsh and grazing. 'Then I suggest, if you don't want men to get the wrong idea, sweetheart, that you don't flutter those pretty lashes quite so enticingly before giving them the brush-off. Fortunately for you, *this* time you've picked on one who can take "no" for an answer. Now, where are you staying on the South Shore?'

Feeling like a child who had been chastised, Lee

gulped, toying with her small cream clutch-bag. Why did he still want to know that?

'I told you. . .I don't want to get involved——'

'You've made that perfectly clear.' The softness with which he spoke emphasised the repressed anger that tautened his jaw, put a hard glitter in his eyes. 'However, I see no point in letting that upset me unduly, and as I happen to be going in that direction anyway, I may as well give you a lift.'

And she was supposed to accept? Get into a car with a man she had been stupid enough to encourage and then turn down flat? Some men couldn't take that sort of rejection. He'd said so himself. And how did she know that, when he'd got her alone in his car, he wouldn't turn out to be one of them? After all, she couldn't really claim to know him from that brief, bitter experience with him before.

'You don't have to,' she responded hastily, looking for a way out of this awkward situation without making a complete fool of herself. She couldn't even tell him she'd decided to go back to the party, as she'd been careless enough to mention that early appointment! 'I can make my own way back.'

'Don't be silly.' His tone reprimanded. 'A cab will cost you, and I have to go that way.'

Goodness! How could she shake him off? Staring at the closed doors of the lift, she racked her brains for a means, fearing not only for her physical safety now, but that he might put two and two together and work out who she was—if he hadn't already. A cold sweat crept over her as she saw him press the lift-button again, impatiently this time. Supposing he was playing his own little game with her? Insisting on taking her home—even though she'd made it clear she didn't want to see him again—because he *knew*! In which case, she didn't doubt that he would take great pleasure in making her pay for that piece of tomfoolery outside.

And then, glancing up, she noticed the sign for the ladies' cloakroom. She could excuse herself, she thought, with a small leap of her heart. Give him the slip that way. Until she remembered that when she'd used the cloakroom earlier she had still had to come back past the lifts. And, no matter how long she was, she had the awful, nagging suspicion that Jordan Colyer would still be waiting for her. Oh, heavens! What could she do?

He had moved over to the terrace doors and was looking out across the harbour when Lee heard voices drawing nearer—people coming up from the ballroom. This was her only chance!

She wasn't certain at first how they could help her, but as they approached a strong instinct for self-preservation had her blurting out in tones loud enough for them to hear, 'If you say you can take "no" for an answer, then why don't you? I've already told you enough times, I'm not interested!'

The look on his face as he swung round was of unutterable disbelief. The others were looking on curiously as they passed, but one middle-aged man stopped, and with an accusing look at Jordan asked, 'Is this chap bothering you?'

Lee shot a wary glance at Jordan. He looked livid! she thought. But, hearing the lift opening, she murmured a tremulous 'yes', darting into it and stabbing at the indicator button, praying the doors would close before Jordan could reach it himself. She heard the stranger's voice raised in challenge against him, and caught her breath as she saw him brush past the other man and stride purposefully towards the lift. But the doors were gliding closed, leaving her only with her shame and her pounding heart, and the startling vision of white-hot fury on Jordan's face, before the hard wall of iron blotted it from view.

CHAPTER TWO

THE sun streaming into the hotel bedroom woke Lee from a dreamless sleep.

Stretching luxuriously, she turned, groaning as the events of the night before suddenly came rushing back to her.

Last night she had behaved shamefully and it had backfired on her, she thought, with her cheeks burning, recalling the way she had led Jordan on, and the look on his face when she had run away from him, leaving those people thinking goodness knew what about him after what she had said!

With a raging remorse, she had to admit that she wouldn't have done that to any man. It was only panic—her desperation at the lifts to get away from him—probably coupled with one Martini too many, she accepted with a grimace, that had made her say what she had.

She shuddered, moving on to her back, trying to gain consolation from telling herself that he deserved it. After all, he hadn't spared *her* feelings eight years ago when he'd been so ready to believe those malicious rumours that she was his father's mistress, had he? she thought bitterly. He'd accused her of leaving Richard to die alone!

Which, dear heaven, she had. But in innocence, she reflected painfully, hands covering her face as those long-buried memories suddenly flooded into her mind.

Complying with her father's last wish that she should go and live with his friend, Richard Colyer, when he died, had seemed the natural thing to do. Her mother had stayed in England after the marriage had broken up, and alone, only seventeen and still a stranger to America, Lee had seen Richard as the uncle figure she'd sorely needed. But when she had moved into his New York home she hadn't realised then just how ill he was himself. Neither had she understood why he had packed her off on that long holiday just a few months later, only afterwards realising that he'd done so to spare her the further trauma of his own death. The first she had known about it was when Jordan had virtually dragged her off that Miami dance-floor; a Jordan she had never met, but whose intruding authority had left her young partner flushed and stammering, the man's hard, phlegmatic command that she should go back to New York with him immediately doing little to conceal the passionate anger behind that external air of control, much less the pain in his grief-clouded eyes. But on that long journey back, in the dark intimacy of his car, she had felt the full whiplash of his anger, his tongue flaying her raw, his harsh conjecture that she was a speculating little tramp suddenly awakening her to the cruel things people had been saying about her and Richard, and to the startling fact that she had inherited a small fortune. As she'd sat beside him, too numb with shock even to cry, Jordan had automatically assumed she didn't care!

'But I wasn't *living* with him. . .not in that way,' she'd denied emphatically, but he'd cut across her desolate words with inexorable brutality.

'There's a name for girls like you,' he'd said, refusing to listen—then or at any time afterwards—his opinions only reinforced by Madeline. Madeline, who had been Richard's assistant and, until then, Lee had thought, her friend.

With a sigh she got up, selecting a green shirtwaister from the wardrobe, recalling, as she moved into the bathroom, how quickly she had left that house, and how Jordan had at least had the decency to try and stop her.

'For goodness' sake, don't be so stubborn-minded! It's your house now, after all.' Under the warm spray of the shower, she remembered his hard, impatient words. 'You've every right to be here. Apart from which, I'd hate to have it on my conscience that I was responsible for a virtual schoolgirl winding up on the streets!'

'Don't worry, Jordan. . .that's not going to happen to me!' she had flung at him, in defence of his unrelenting attitude towards her, and wished she hadn't when her assertion had given him the cue to hurt her even more.

'No. . .my father paid very handsomely for the privilege of your. . .favours, didn't he?' he had said abrasively. 'If one can call it a privilege.' Coldly, that dark gaze had run over her body, a hard, insolent male appraisal that had made her cheeks flame. 'Personally, I'd have thought he'd have preferred something a little more developed, but no doubt you'll find some other rich sucker eager enough to take you into his bed.'

A self-conscious teenager, still sensitive about her appearance, his cruel criticism of her figure had cut her to the quick. She had been attracted to him, too—unbelievably so—she remembered poignantly, which was why those barbed words and his continual refusal to believe her had succeeded in hurting her so much. Alone and afraid, she had almost broken down and cried in front of him then. For a few moments, recognising mutual grief in him behind his censuring hatred, she had wanted to sob out her heart. Feel his arms around her, someone who was contact with Richard and, indirectly, her father. But she hadn't dared. He had been too unapproachable, and she had had too much pride. Instead, she had drawn herself up to her full height—which even now was still somewhere short of his shoulder—and, lifting her young, tortured face to his, had responded insurgently, 'That's right—I will!' She'd realised then, as now, as she towelled herself dry, that that last foolish statement had probably cemented his opinion of her for good.

She breakfasted in the dining-room, without Vince, who, she assumed, was still in bed, although she would have given anything for his company this morning. She needed something, she felt, to ease her burning self-recrimination over the way she'd behaved last night, though gradually the bright warm Bermuda day helped.

A white meshwork of apartments, this part of the hotel overlooked the Great Sound, the glittering blue water with its cluster of bobbing boats and tiny islands, and the cry of sea-birds drifting in through the open windows, soothing and relaxing her, so that she felt much more composed by the time she was due to leave for her appointment.

Locking her door, she turned, gasping as she almost collided with someone.

'Vince!'

In shabby jeans and a checked shirt, he looked his usual unruffled self, though he threw up his hands in defence when he saw the accusation on Lee's face.

'All right! All right! I know I was supposed to come up for you last night, and I did.' He shrugged when he saw her frown.

'Well, at half-past, anyway,' he clarified then. 'I thought I'd give you an extra half an hour with that guy. But I was only thinking of you,' he added hastily, hurrying after her down the carpeted corridor as she swung away from him with an air of not altogether mock disdain. 'I thought that if a guy like that couldn't interest you in a bit of the rare old passion and moonlight—no one could.'

'Thanks, Vince.' Lee shot a glance at his rather rangy figure, her sigh exasperated. 'With friends like you, I can do without enemies.'

'Why? You're not telling me you let him get away, are you?' He followed her into the waiting lift, the doors closing behind them, and Lee's stomach lurched as she thought of that other lift, in that other hotel. 'Hey! I didn't upset the old apple-cart too much by not coming up on time, did I?'

He looked genuinely repentant, probably noticing how pale she'd gone, she thought, and she managed a wan smile, shaking her dark head. Perhaps Jordan's pride was smarting this morning, but, as bad as she felt about the way she had acted, there was no real harm done. Besides, she had no wish to think about the man, let alone discuss him. There were more important issues on her mind right now, like the appointment with Mason, and she conveyed as much to Vince.

'Where men are concerned, everything's more important,' he said somewhat censuringly. 'Honestly, Lee, sometimes I think that self-sufficiency has become an obsession with you.'

She checked the retort which sprang to her lips, considering how near the truth his words might be. Well, what if they were? she ruminated, staring at the indicator panel with a line drawing her fine, velvety brows together. Hadn't she made a vow to herself that she would never be like her mother?

Laconically, though, she uttered, 'That's right,' just as the doors glided apart on the ground floor. 'And *you* make sure you don't become too obsessed with the scenery here—particularly the two-legged variety——' she interposed lightly, pulling a face '—to remember that some time during this working holiday I might require you for the services you're being paid very generously for.'

'You're the boss.'

She left him in the lift, saluting her, and despite **every**thing—last night, Jordan, the problems with the magazine—she couldn't contain the small ripple of amusement Vince always stirred in her as she hurried out to the waiting taxi.

The industrialist's home was a stately mansion on the very edge of the ocean, Lee discovered, where a native, grey-haired manservant immediately ushered her into the garden. Perfect green lawns stood against a riot of colour, though her attention was drawn sharply to the elderly man who was sitting in a wheelchair on the patio.

'What's the matter? Haven't you seen a cripple before?' he queried impatiently, making Lee embarrassingly conscious of how startled she must have looked. But justifiably, she felt, since the last time she'd read anything about him he'd been referred to as 'an active and sport-loving tycoon'.

'The result of a riding accident,' he went on to enlighten her, dismissing the other man. 'However, my physiotherapist has great hopes for me, so I'm told.' A hard mouth compressed above a strong, forceful jaw. 'Be that as it may, you won't be writing about that. . .if indeed I allow you to write anything at all.'

Beneath the shirtwaister, Lee stiffened, her hands tensing around her matching green bag. He had to be sixty plus, but there was an autocratic strength in that rugged face in spite of his disability. A man renowned for the number of women on the boards of his companies, he had seemed a stimulating subject for the *Apple*'s mainly female readership, and the journal desperately needed some new stimulus if it were to survive. But he was doing a very good job of reminding her that he was the sought-after commodity here—of exactly where she stood with him, which was nowhere at this precise moment, she was quick to caution herself.

'I can assure you, I've no intention of prying into your private affairs, Mr Mason,' she uttered sweetly, as she knew what this story was worth to her magazine.

She started when he shot back, 'You're darn right, you won't!' He laughed loudly when he saw her flinch, his laughter echoed by the sudden raucous chattering of a kiskadee somewhere in the garden. 'You print one word I don't agree with, and I'll see to it you never print another.' It was an intimidating threat, but the sudden twinkling of brilliant blue eyes told her that even *he* knew he was overstepping the boundaries of his influence with that one. She began to suspect his bark was far worse than his bite.

The hiss of the ocean filled the moment's silence—varying and eternal beyond the gentle slope of the lawns.

'May I ask why you agreed to see me at all,' she queried candidly, 'since you're obviously so averse to the idea of being interviewed?' She knew she was lucky even seeing him at all, but she couldn't help letting him know that she wasn't one to be browbeaten, and from the rather surprised look on that authoritative face she had achieved her objective.

'I had my reasons,' he said rather evasively, 'not the least of which being that I admire ambition, Miss Roman, particularly in a woman.' He gestured impatiently towards one of the ornate iron chairs which complemented a matching garden-table, and Lee complied, sitting down. 'For someone your age to head a concern like *Eve's Apple* it must have taken a hell of a lot of guts. Or money.' Unaccountably she flinched as, with a deftness born of long practice, he manoeuvred his chair so that he could look at her without the sun in his eyes, the wheels making a high-pitched squeak over the grey stone flags. 'Rumour has it that you started that magazine at the age of nineteen.' He was studying her obliquely, her cool, unruffled poise, her wind-teased hair and her clear, steady gaze, and he shook his head as though he had a job coming to terms with what he saw. 'Care to tell me how you did it?'

It was a conspiratorial whisper, curiosity etching features which were weathered bronze beneath a crop of silver hair.

Lee smiled, her cool gaze giving nothing away. 'Just sheer hard work,' she said simply, because it had been. 'I saw the opening for a magazine geared at the modern woman in New York, and jumped in. And I hardly need to tell a man like you what little miracles can happen with knowing the right people, and with the right sort of finance,' she added lightly. But she didn't elaborate that, if she couldn't pull off some sort of major miracle soon, all her hard-won efforts might well have been for nothing.

Her reply seemed to satisfy him, and, following her gaze to the tree where the kiskadee chattered, he said, 'Well. . .what do you think of my retreat?'

Appreciatively, Lee looked around her. The splendour of the house spoke for itself, with its rambling architecture and stark white roof, while the deepest crimson of a climbing bougainvillaea lent colour to its pastel walls. Steps led away from the patio, as did the gradual descent of a ramp, a recent addition, Lee

assumed at once, to enable Alec Mason ease of man-
oeuvrability to the gardens and the vivid, sparkling
waters of the pool.

'It's lovely.'

The man's mouth compressed in satisfaction. 'I'm
glad you think so, because I've had a room prepared
for you for the duration of the time it takes to do these
infernal interviews.'

So he was actually agreeing to them, if not rather
begrudgingly!

'That's very considerate of you. . .but not necessary,' Lee declined, rather taken aback by his offer of
accommodation. 'I've already booked rooms at a hotel
with the photographer for——'

'Then tell them you've made other plans.' Mason
swung his chair to face Lee squarely, impatience out-
lined in the tautness of his jaw. 'If I'm to be given
publicity, then I want to know who by, and I can't get
to know my interviewer if I'm immoblised here and
she's in some hotel miles out of reach! I value my
privacy too much, young woman, to sell it to a perfect
stranger, no matter how admirable a businesswoman
she is.' He moved, and now that his face was in full
sunshine Lee could see the weary lines that etched it.
Behind that brusque, hard-bitten exterior, she realised,
was a tired, ageing man fighting the frustration of his
incapacity—and alone, since it was common knowledge that he had never married. She felt a sudden tug
of sympathy for him.

'I understand,' she said, with a gentle smile. 'It's just
that I didn't want to impose——'

'You're a liar, Miss Roman.' A deep, disparaging
voice brought her head round sharply, had her blanch-
ing at the sight of the man who had just come out of
the house. Pure, cold fear brought her tongue flicking

across her lips, one glance at those hard, implacable features assuring her that Jordan Colyer was relishing her alarm. 'Isn't imposition the fundamental art of journalism?'

Cool mockery threaded his tones, that strong sexual aura the man radiated somehow intensified in the hard brilliance of day. He looked dynamic, forceful and superbly elegant, the powerful lines of his body enhanced by a lightweight, tailored suit. The glimmer of satisfaction in his eyes, though, made Lee's stomach clench sickeningly. What was he going to say—or do? she wondered, her heart hammering crazily. Had he realised who she really was? Futilely, she wished that whatever force was behind the Bermuda Triangle would come to her aid now, and make her disappear.

In a cold sweat, she heard Alec Mason introduce him as his nephew. 'Jordan's work covers everything from timber to high technology,' his uncle was conveying proudly, 'although it doesn't bring him here quite as often as I'd like. However, he's combining business with a holiday this time, so we can expect to see a lot of him while he's here.'

Rigid with fear, Lee looked up at the man towering above her, her mouth moving stiffly—tremulously—into something that didn't quite reach a smile. His own was polite, and he appeared remarkably cool and unperturbed. If she had got to him last night, she thought, with a small shiver, he was above letting it show in front of his uncle.

'Well. . .this trip will indeed prove interesting. . .particularly if *you're* staying here.' She could feel the contempt behind that innate charm as those dark, penetrating eyes seemed to skewer her to her chair. 'However, don't let my uncle bully you into it.' He dropped a glance to the man in the wheelchair, his features classically striking in profile. 'Who knows, Alec?' A muscle twitched at the corner of his nephew's mouth. 'Perhaps Miss Roman has. . .personal reasons for preferring the formality of a hotel.'

Meaning that she probably enjoyed her little game of seducing and humiliating the guests!

Utterly abashed, she felt her colour rise, and berated herself for not connecting him with Mason before she'd acted so stupidly with him last night. After all, there was a family resemblance about that mouth and prominent jaw, and in that deep, Canadian drawl.

Telling herself she had no one to blame but herself, she forced her lips to imitate a smile. 'I never respond to bullying, Mr Colyer.' And, hanging on to some shred of the confidence which was rapidly deserting her, she added, 'As I'm sure Mr Mason's discovered about me already.'

Against the interminable wash of the ocean, she heard the older man grunt. 'Outspoken, isn't she?' he complained, although she noticed an indefinable gleam of something in the glance he exchanged with his nephew. 'One of these modern young women who knows what she wants and gets it. More the type you're used to, Jordan, rather than a worn-out old bachelor like me. Think you could handle her?'

They were discussing her as if she were a recalcitrant child, Lee thought rebelliously, mortified to hear the older man's suggestion, and, risking a glance up at Jordan, saw him smile with all the complacency of a cat that had just cornered a shrew.

'The pleasure will be all mine, Alec.' The meaningful softness with which he said it sent a little tremor down Lee's spine. What exactly did he intend to do? she wondered, goose-pimples prickling over her flesh. And if he did remember her—what then?

Her nostrils caught the faint, masculine scent of him as he moved, her insurgent gaze faltering beneath the hard smugness of his. Legs slightly apart, hands thrust deep into his trouser pockets, the very casualness of his stance seemed to emphasise his complete command of the situation, and Lee felt hot colour creeping up her throat from remembering how it felt to be held against the warm strength of him, the touch of those lips that she had so shamefully invited. . .

'Well?'

His deep voice brought her out of her disturbing reverie to realise that she was virtually alone with him now. Almost without her being aware of it, the other man had wheeled himself away through the open patio doors into the house. So this was it—the moment of reckoning, she thought, with a sick contraction of her stomach, and got to her feet so as not to feel so overshadowed by his dominating height.

'Well, what?' she queried cagily, her breath locking in her chest, her lips compressed against that wholly feminine part of herself that acknowledged Jordan Colyer as a man.

The hard mouth quirked, curled slightly in sadistic enjoyment of her unease. 'Are you going to avail yourself of my uncle's hospitality, or are you going to return to New York empty-handed? Because I don't think I need to point out that if you don't meet him on his terms, there'll be no interviews.'

And he'd suggested that she shouldn't let his *uncle* bully her! Breathing again—almost faint with relief—she nearly told him then to stick his interviews—that this story about his uncle was hardly life and death to her magazine. But it could well be, she reminded herself frustratedly, and besides, allowing him to think he'd browbeaten her into leaving would be like handing him satisfaction on a plate. So, lifting her small chin and flashing him a saccharine smile, she said in honeyed tones, 'Put like that, Mr Colyer, how can I refuse?'

A dark eyebrow lifted at the unmistakable sarcasm, but his gaze had fallen to the smooth line of her throat, rested on the gently pulsing hollow, almost as if he had registered that absurd quickening in its rhythm. But he said simply, 'Good,' and, sending a glance towards the house, 'You'll have to make allowances for my uncle, of course.' Concern cut a furrow across the high, intellectual forehead. 'I'm afraid his immobility has made him unusually churlish and impatient, but he's all the family I've got and I'm very fond of him, so see that you don't upset him any more than you have to.'

And that was *it?* Flabbergasted, she couldn't believe she had been let off so lightly, because now he was issuing instructions to the Bermudian he called Matthew, who had just come out again with a tray, to arrange for a cab to take her back to the hotel.

'I'd take you myself, but I've got an appointment in the opposite direction in precisely. . .fifteen minutes,' Jordan told her, consulting the gold watch beneath an immaculate white cuff. 'No doubt I'll see you later,' he said drily, and strode away.

Her relief was immense as she watched him go, and with weak knees she flopped down on to her chair, staring absently at the dark coffee being poured. What was wrong with the man? Why hadn't he said something when he'd had the chance? she wondered suspiciously. Or did he think it best to forget the whole incident beyond making her sweat a bit? Optimistically, she preferred to believe that that was the case, and had started to feel a little more relaxed by the time Alec joined her again.

* * *

Vince wasn't at the hotel when Lee returned. Scribbling him a note, which she left with the desk-clerk, she packed her belongings, then telephoned Rachael, her secretary back in New York, to let her know where she would be.

'Last month's figures came through, and they look pretty grim again,' the other woman mentioned with less than her usual effervescence. 'I've got the print-out here somewhere. . .' There was a pause, where Lee envisaged her rummaging through an untidy basket of 'matters pending' on an equally disorganised desk. But Rachael was efficient, in spite of it, the same age as Lee and a good friend, and Lee often wondered what she would do without her secretary. 'Ah, here it is. . .'

Rachael hadn't exaggerated. April's figures were depressing, and staff morale was taking a dive, Lee realised, just from listening to her secretary's tone. She knew she owed it to them to keep the magazine thriving, or consider selling out, she thought, coming off the phone. But for the past six years she had put everything she had into *Eve's Apple*—mentally, physically and financially—and she didn't think she could bear it if she lost her magazine, the foundations of which had been laid unknowingly by her father, with the rocky little printing business he'd left her. She had tears in her eyes as she rang for a taxi to take her back to the house.

'Mr Mason's still having his physiotherapy,' a maid told her, letting her in, 'but he's asked me to show you your room.' And, seeing Lee struggling with her suitcase and a portable typewriter, the girl advised, 'Leave the case here in the hall. I'll get one of the men to bring it up for you later.'

Grateful, Lee did as she suggested, then followed her upstairs.

The room she was shown into was more luxurious than anything she could have expected in even the best hotel, with its beautiful inlaid furniture, rose-velvet curtains and matching deep-pile carpet. A tastefully contrasting duvet graced the double bed, while the modern conveniences of an en suite bathroom provided all the necessities and comforts she would have found in her own New York apartment, except that here she could hear the sea from the bedroom window and the musical 'churlee' of a bluebird, while from somewhere in the garden came the oscillating whine of a lawn-mower.

She was freshening up in the bathroom when the telephone shrilled beside her bed.

'Just when I thought you and I were going to get better acquainted,' Vince began without any preamble when Lee answered it, 'and what do you do? Move out of the hotel.' She heard him chuckling on the other end of the line. 'Rumours are that Mason's got an eye for a pretty woman,' he went on to say. 'No wonder he's asked you to stay. Or have you met the magnificent, all-powerful nephew and been smitten enough to whee-dle the invitation yourself?'

His reference to Jordan surprised her, and she stared at the receiver suspiciously. 'You didn't tell me he had a nephew,' she commented, her tone almost accusing as she wondered if he'd known all along that it was Jordan she'd behaved so outrageously with the pre-vious night. It was the sort of situation that would have amused Vince immensely.

'Dark, charismatic, and quite irresistible as far as women are concerned, I'm told, though I've never actually met the man personally,' she heard him saying, and felt instantly ashamed of her immediate and very incorrect deductions. 'He's a powerful name in business though, worth millions before he was thirty. He's keen-witted, clever, and the type who would make a danger-ous adversary. I've also heard he carries a lot of influence with Mason, and I've also seen you instantly rebel against his particular type, so if you do meet him, don't get on the wrong side of him, will you, ol' girl?'

A fine perspiration broke out on Lee's skin. If only Vince knew!

'Look, about these photographs. . .' With a queasy feeling in her stomach she changed the subject, unable to bring herself to enlighten Vince that she had already made an enemy of the great Jordan Colyer last night—and for the second time! She only wished she'd never gone to that party—never even come to Bermuda. She would have given anything never to have laid eyes on him again.

A knock at her door had her guessing that it was her luggage arriving, and glancing over her shoulder she stiffened when, on her verbal response, the door opened to admit not Matthew, the Bermudian, as she'd thought, but Jordan, carrying her case.

'Thanks,' she uttered curtly, as he put it down, and dismissively she turned away to wind up her conversa-tion with the photographer. Her relief was almost audible as she heard the door click closed, but when she turned round she realised that Jordan hadn't left as she'd thought, but was leaning against the door with his arms folded, watching her.

CHAPTER THREE

Lee's face grew pale against the dark, feathered layers of her hair. 'W—what do you want?' she faltered, fear coiling inside her.

'I think you know.'

The grim pull of Jordan's lips caused a painful tightening in her stomach, and nervously her fingers toyed with the top buttons of her dress. 'Get out.'

He ignored her breathless command, dropping his arms to his sides and coming away from the door with a lazy insolence that made her pulses thud. His jacket and tie had been discarded, and the almost transparent quality of his shirt alluded to the sinewy strength of him, while the shadow of dark hair spanning his chest screamed of a virility that had Lee touching her tongue to her lips.

'That was a pretty low-down thing you did to me last night.' His tone, and the gaze that flicked contemptuously over her, burned with a controlled anger. 'I don't know what little game you thought you were playing, but it wasn't too funny from the side I was on. I had a tough job convincing that crowd I wasn't some sort of sex maniac.' There was an odd quirk to his lips. 'Still, I suppose it's no more than can be expected from the mother of that feminist rag you call a magazine. What's wrong, Lee. . .don't you like men?'

His fingers were splayed against his hips, the hard cast of his features causing her throat to constrict painfully. Annoyed, though, by the way he'd referred to *Eve's Apple*, she snapped, 'It's not a rag—it's a

voice for women. And one I don't like to curb with
unnecessary censure or editing. Perhaps it's you with
the problem, Jordan.' She tilted her head to regard
him with cool, challenging eyes, her slight frame
making her look oddly young against the hard, mature
strength of his. 'What's wrong?' she taunted, deliberately mimicking his own question. 'Finding it hard
coming to terms with the equality of the sexes?'

There was a soft sound against the window as an
unsuspecting moth hit the hard pane.

'Oh, I'm for equality,' he said drily. 'Up to the hilt.
But it doesn't rule out respect—on either side. And
I'm sorry to say, little lady, that you need teaching
some.'

The distinct threat in his voice had Lee backing
away, only to find her progress halted by the solid
barrier of the dressing-table. 'Don't you touch me!'

Her eyes flashed a warning as he kept on coming,
and she gave a small gasp when he moved to imprison
her with a hand on either side of the dressing-table, so
that she almost fell back on to it in order to avoid
actually touching him.

'That wasn't the message you were giving me last
night.'

His rasped reminder brought instant colour to her
cheeks. 'Last night I'd had too much to drink,' she
uttered, in a vain attempt to excuse her shameful
behaviour, her breasts rising and falling sharply, and
her senses swimming, from the intimidating threat of
his nearness.

His mouth moved in hard contemplation. 'And you
think that justifies leading a man on, and then trying to
ruin his reputation when you've grown bored with him
an hour later?'

'Let me go!'

He had caught the hands which were suddenly trying to push him away, pinning them behind her back in just one of his, to say grimly, 'Not this time, Lee.' His expression was inexorable. 'Just thank your lucky stars you aren't a few years younger, or I might have been tipping you across my knee now. However, as you're way past the age of consent and well aware of what your little game was leading to last night, I'll simply take some of what you were offering in compensation.'

'No!' It was a small, panicked sound, silenced beneath the bruising pressure of his mouth. His lips demanded, forcing hers to part with a determination that sought only to punish, his strong, masculine jaw grazing the more delicate structure of hers.

She had never been kissed with such angry single-mindedness in her life, her breasts crushed against the hard, unyielding wall of his chest as his arm locked her to him with none of the tenderness he had shown her the night before. There was a controlled expertise, though, in the way his tongue probed the sweet, hidden recesses of her mouth, a sexual sophistication that excited her even as she fought against it, and which had her struggling harder to get away from him, her incautious movements bringing her into even closer proximity with his muscular strength, so that he laughed deep in his throat.

His free hand was making light work of the buttons on her dress, his hard fingers splaying across the lace of her bra to cup the soft, warm mound it covered. She gave a small, guttural sound of protest against the intimacy, hating him, and the sudden traitorous response of her breast as it burgeoned beneath his palm filled her with a mixture of revulsion and anger, and such sick, sick desire. . .

No!

Almost as if she had screamed that rejection of her thoughts aloud, he was letting her go, and disgustedly she staggered back from him, her hand against her mouth. Dazedly, her senses began to register the sound of the lawn-mower again, and the smell of freshly cut grass, and, worse, the cool smugness in Jordan's eyes as they took in her flushed cheeks and kiss-swollen lips, the irregularity of her breathing.

'Not bad,' he commented derisively then. 'But, from the games you play, I was expecting something a little more practised.'

A query darkened his eyes with a cool cognisance of the self-abasement in hers, so that she hissed at him, 'Get out!'

This time he complied, but turned at the door, his hand on the knob, to say quietly, 'Now I think we're equal in the humiliation stakes, Lee.'

And he'd enjoyed ramming that point home, she realised with a burning self-disgust, because nothing could have been more humiliating than the knowledge of her body's response to him just now. But had he been fully aware of it? she wondered, cheeks flaming from the liberty he had taken with her. Known that, physically, she'd been in danger of wanting him as much as he had wanted her? Because when he'd kissed her, she reflected tensely, heat suffusing her slender body as she hauled her suitcase up on to the bed, there had been no question—in spite of his anger—that he'd been aroused. Her only comfort as she started to unpack lay in the thought that, now he'd had his moment of satisfaction, he'd probably be very unlikely to come near her again.

'Massey's got a heart of gold,' Arlene Davidson, a chatty, no-nonsense brunette of around fortyish, told

Lee the following morning. 'Even if he does seem like a grumpy old beggar.' They were sitting, feet dangling, on the edge of the pool, watching Alec exercising with the aid of floats in the sparkling water, and the therapist cast a glance over her shoulder at the magnificent house, grimacing at Lee. 'Rather a poor choice of phrase, I'm afraid,' she laughed. 'The man's made of it!'

Lee smiled in response, liking the woman, and contentedly she tipped her head back to feel the warm Bermuda sunshine on her face. She was sharing this therapy session because Alec had insisted she be there; because he had said that he felt at less of a disadvantage—less of a cripple—in the water, telling her to bring her notebook and pen. And this morning he had talked freely, about his past life, his business ventures, the near failures and inevitable successes, and the role of women in his varied commercial enterprises. He had talked to Lee, and Lee alone, as though Arlene were not there, although the therapist hadn't seemed to mind, only chipping in when she felt he wasn't taking full advantage of the water, sometimes reprimanding him for not listening to her with a brusqueness that matched his own, and which had Lee turning away to hide her amusement.

'What do you think of the nephew?' Arlene was sipping a glass of fruit juice, the pure orange liquid a striking contrast against the stark black of her swimsuit. 'Bit of a heart-throb, isn't he? If I were ten years younger I'd snap him up before somebody else did, although Massey seems to think he's nicely tied up with that secretary of his in New York.'

Lee shifted uncomfortably, glancing away to hide her unease. So even the mature, unmarried Arlene wasn't immune to that breath-catching magnetism, she realised, surprised, but managed to answer with feigned casualness, 'Is he? I hadn't really noticed.' But, finding herself wondering what Jordan's choice of woman was like, she pulled her thoughts up sharply. What the hell did she care? When this job was through here, hopefully she'd never have to set eyes on the man again, and she could think herself fortunate that she'd only had to suffer a few moments of his company since that little episode yesterday.

He hadn't been at lunch—or dinner. Alec had said he'd been engaged in some business in Hamilton, and she'd been enjoying a liqueur with her host in the sumptuous, Colonial-style drawing-room, laughing at some little joke he had made, when Jordan had suddenly strode in. His gaze had been unfathomable as it had flicked from Lee to his uncle, and back to Lee again, while Alec had said jovially, 'I think I've been wrong all these years decrying the entire breed of journalists, Jordan. This one's enlightening!' Then, to her surprise, he'd reached across and squeezed her hand hard, adding, 'It might be a trick of the trade, but she certainly knows how to bring an old invalid out of himself.'

The genuine warmth in those twinkling eyes had made her smile, because although she hadn't intentionally set out to use any wiles—either feminine or professional—to make him warm towards her, she'd been glad that she'd helped him to do so, sensing that he didn't relax easily with people, especially since his accident, which, she had learned, had been eighteen months before.

Jordan, however, she reflected, had been suitably unimpressed. 'I'd be careful, Alec,' he'd drawled, pouring himself a drink from the sideboard. 'Such beauty could well induce a man to give away far more than he ever intended.'

Beneath his cool examination, she had felt the hard throb of her pulse, and even now, in the brightness of day, Lee shuddered, finding his remark too synonymous with the past. But it had been pure coincidence, she tried to impress upon herself for the umpteenth time since last night. He didn't know who she was. . .did he?

'Oh, well. . .I think that's enough for one morning.' Arlene's practical tones brought Lee's attention back to the poolside. The woman was helping her patient out of the water by means of a battery-operated lift at one side of the pool: the most difficult procedure was transferring him from the raised platform to his chair, Lee realised, because the industrialist was a big man, and quickly she went to Arlene's aid.

'Good girl,' Arlene applauded breathlessly, when they had got a robe around Alec and he was seated safely back in the wheelchair. 'I usually get one of the staff to help me, but you've a natural way with people that everyone hasn't got. Ever considered nursing?'

Watching Arlene position the chair under the shade of a poinciana tree, Lee shook her head. 'I always wanted to go into journalism, although I did nurse my father for a time before he died,' she admitted softly, deciding that it was safe to divulge that much about herself in front of Alec. After all, Richard had been his late sister's husband, she had learned quite innocently yesterday, and she wasn't sure how much her host knew about the girl who had lived with his brother-in-law for those few months, or what his own opinion of her was. Totally unfavourable, no doubt, if he'd listened to Jordan, she thought grievously, struck with a pang of guilt about unintentionally having to deceive

Alec. She was beginning to like him. 'I admire the medical profession immensely,' she expressed, remembering the feeling of total helplessness she'd known when her father had had his heart attack, 'but I really don't think I'd have been cut out for the job.' She laughed, adding with a little shudder, 'All those needles and bedpans!'

'Pity.' They both looked questioningly towards Alec, who was unfolding a newspaper beneath the flamboyant scarlet of the poinciana, and directing a grimace at Arlene. 'She's got a much gentler touch than you.'

'Then I've obviously missed out somewhere.' Lee swung round as Jordan's deep tones intruded upon the conversation. He was standing just behind her, looking coolly amused, a dark jacket slung over one shoulder, those brown eyes assessing her figure with such naked insolence that she blushed, wishing she was wearing a practical, sexless-looking one-piece like the other woman, instead of her skimpy white bikini with its beaded strings. 'Still, they say the softer the kitten, the sharper the claws, Alec, so perhaps you'd best stick with Arlene.'

No one else noticed that steely edge to his voice, Lee realised, hearing the therapist's chuckle and Alec's dissatisfied grunt. It was a private communication for her ears only, but without giving him the satisfaction of even a glance, Lee grabbed her notebook from her sun-lounger and made to follow Alec as he began wheeling himself away.

'Going in already?' Jordan sounded surprised. 'And I was hoping to join you all in the pool.'

Lee couldn't help hugging a secret pleasure to herself that he was too late, and was so immersed in the feeling that she almost collided with Alec's chair as he pulled up unexpectedly in front of her.

'Arlene tells me I've had enough for today, and you know how bossy she is.' Silver hair caught the sunlight as he pulled a wry face at Jordan, while the woman stood beside the wheelchair looking resignedly amused. 'However, I've finished with this young lady. . .for the moment anyway. . .' To Lee's utter dismay, Alec was gesturing in her direction. 'I'm sure she'd be delighted to join you.'

Against the soft sibilance of the ocean, Lee drew a sharp, almost audible breath. Jordan was looking down at her, his features inscrutable, save for the smallest twitch of amusement playing around his mouth. And at her expense, she thought, feeling she would rather die than spend any time alone with him—and he knew it!

'I'd like to stay,' she lied, for Alec's benefit, 'but I've got to get these typed up——'

'There's plenty of time for that.' A disparaging hand dismissed the notebook Lee was clutching like a life-line. 'Stay with Jordan. Have some fun. You can get your typing done when the sun goes down.'

Alec was being considerate—she knew that—yet she took his deep recommendation with a sinking feeling. If she made too much fuss about staying out here, Jordan might well start to get suspicious about her—if he wasn't already, after her behaviour the other night, she thought uneasily—so to comply seemed the only thing to do.

'I'll see you in five minutes, then,' he drawled, his eyes glimmering with the hard light of triumph when he saw the mutinous spark in hers. In fact, he was back in less, surprising her with the speed at which he had changed.

She was already in the water, working off her

frustration at being left virtually no choice about joining him, and pretended not to notice him as he came up to the poolside. In truth, that superb muscular torso hadn't escaped her quickly averted eyes, and she had had an immediate impression of power and strength rippling through a body that was lean and hard and tanned, and clad now only in a pair of dark bathing-trunks.

'I thought you wanted to swim!' she called out rather pointedly after a few moments, because he was still standing there, and though she was a proficient swimmer she was beginning to feel awkward and clumsy with him watching her.

Without a word he took the cue, his body breaking the surface of the water with a deep plunge that sent a quiver of apprehension along Lee's spine. But she need not have worried. He made no attempt to come near her, immediately breaking into a powerful front crawl, that driving stamina carrying him through the water with admirable ease. For lap after lap they swam apart and in silence, until eventually, gliding through the water to the end where the sun-loungers were, Lee saw Jordan easing himself out. She stopped, just a yard or so away from him, letting her feet touch the bottom, but he turned and saw her standing there, flushed and breathless, her breasts lifting sharply as she tried to regain her breath.

'Here.' He extended a hand to help her out, that bronzed body glistening all over with tiny droplets of water. Like a sun-god, she thought fancifully, adorned with hundreds of silver beads. Unwilling, though, to share any physical contact with him—however brief— she was twisting away and plunging back into the cool depths. She'd swim up and back again if it killed her, she determined, if that was the only way to avoid him.

But before she had even reached the other end, she felt the first grip of cramp so unexpectedly in her calf muscle that she had to pull herself out, then realised how ridiculous she must look. Now he'd know why she'd swum away like that, she thought hopelessly.

He was towelling his hair, one foot resting on one of the sun-beds, dark hairs clinging damply to his chest and powerful legs. But then suddenly his actions stopped as abruptly as a cut film as he turned and saw her walking towards him.

He looked faintly amused at first. Probably because he knew just how much she had wanted to avoid touching him, she thought sheepishly. But then his expression changed. There was a tautness to the hard structure of his face—partially shaded by the poinciana—such hungry fascination in the gaze that tugged down over the slim, lithe contours of her body that Lee felt something electric run through the air that separated them. She licked her lips, wanting to look away, and couldn't, somehow mesmerised by the dark influence of the man who was watching her.

'What's wrong?' she challenged lightly, although there was a little tremor in her voice, because now, as she approached him, she could feel a tension in him, so tangible, it seemed to reach out and touch her. 'Haven't you ever seen a woman in a bikini before?'

Her words seemed to disperse that uneasy tension. She took a steadying breath, saw Jordan's body almost visibly relax, that cool amusement return to pull at the corners of his mouth.

'Many times.' This was said with a deliberate and more calculated assessment of her moderate breasts, narrow waist and rather curvy hips—a look that heated her skin and told her he was fully in command of himself again—before he added, 'Just never in one so delightfully see-through.'

'Ooh!' Appalled, Lee swiftly brought her arms up across her breasts, realising how stupid she had been. The bikini's label warned of the possibility of it becoming transparent when wet, but it was one she wore only to sunbathe—like this morning—when she hadn't intended to swim. In her confusion, when Alec had insisted she stay with Jordan, she hadn't given it a second thought. And now he'd watched her walk the entire length of the poolside as good as naked!

Looking anxiously about her for something to put round herself, she heard his soft laugh, then felt the damp, sun-warmed towel he'd been using cover her shoulders. It smelt of chlorine, mingling with the musky, male scent of his body.

She gasped as he caught her, turning her to face him, ignoring the warning in her sea-green eyes.

'It's all right, little Eve. . .there's only the two of us. . .and I didn't mind one bit.' There was a deep, sensual quality to his voice that had her biting her lower lip. 'Tell me something, Lee.' With a cool clarity he surveyed the damp, dark hair, the soft curvature of her forehead, and her wide mouth beneath the eyes that held a glittering challenge to his, and the thick masculine brows drew together. 'Have we met before?'

Lee's stomach churned sickeningly as a light breeze lifted the leaves of the poinciana. She shrugged, trying to appear unperturbed. 'I hardly think so,' she retorted, fearing his reaction if he did guess the truth. 'And that's hardly an original line!'

Her chin lifted with a cool hauteur, which was repaid with a tightening of his hands on her upper arms when she would have swung away from him.

Afraid, Lee pushed at him, and, feeling that shock

of wiry hair beneath her fingers, let her hands fall as if he were radioactive. 'Let me go!'

He laughed humourlessly at her instant withdrawal, and the two spots of angry colour high on her cheeks. 'No,' he stated, phlegmatically, his aroused temper held in check by that cool self-command. 'Not until you tell me why you're constantly so determined to antagonise me—why you're afraid of me, Lee.' His voice had grown deceptively soft. 'Because you are.'

Lee's throat contracted. He was too perceptive by half!

Her lips parting, she tried to say something, and couldn't, too unsettled by his nearness, that raw sexuality he oozed. The sun shining down through the poinciana gilded his body with mosaic gold, dappled shadows speckling his skin with all the sinewy, dangerous beauty of a serpent's.

'I didn't read those signals incorrectly the other night,' he said quietly, the hands that rested on her shoulders sending unwelcome sensations through her. 'My antennae aren't so wrongly attuned to have miscalculated those shock-waves coming across that dancefloor. So why did you give me the brush-off when things started getting a bit heated?' His head tilted, his hair like polished jet above the high sweep of his brow. 'Afraid of what you were feeling? Or is that oversensitive womanhood of yours too affronted to admit that you were actually enjoying it?'

She looked at him warily, her lips tightening in selfdisgust, because she had liked it. But what little selfrespect must she have to welcome the advances of a man she despised—who, in truth, despised her? she asked herself, ashamed.

'You're really the most conceited——' She broke off, lost for a more suitable adjective to describe him, and at the same time alleviate her own degradation in being so aware of him. 'Perhaps your deduction was right yesterday,' she attempted to convince him tartly. 'Perhaps I just don't like men!' Adding, when he offered a smile of infuriating mockery, 'Anyway, it might interest you to know that they're not all like you.'

'Obviously not.'

His succinct reply had her looking at him puzzlingly, regretting that she had got herself into such a heated and disconcerting exchange with him. 'Oh?'

His mouth pulled down one side. 'You've been here less than twenty-four hours, and yet you've become friendly enough with Alec to have him eating out of your hand. Not bad, when his first reaction to your wanting a story was a definite refusal. I would have thought, at the very least, that I'd be entitled to some thanks, if not the same respect, after all my efforts to get him to see you.'

Lee stared at him as he picked up his wristwatch from the table between the sun-beds, his movements easy and fluid. 'What do you mean. . .*your* efforts?' she queried, brushing a stray hair out of her eyes. 'Alec said——'

'Oh, he was very impressed with your youth and achievement,' he supplied for her, as if he had known what she had been about to say. 'But you don't really think that would have been enough to get you into his house, do you? He hasn't given an interview in years!' She watched him fix the strap to his wrist, jerking it into place. 'Believe me, it took a lot of persuading on my part to get him to agree to see you at all.'

Lee frowned, her eyes searching those well-sculpted features, taking in the strength of character in that aristocratic nose and thrusting jaw, in the almost chiselled line of his mouth. Really he was quite devastating, she thought absently, unable to prevent her gaze from slipping to his shoulders, to the deep, muscular velvet of his chest. . .

'Why?' she quizzed, looking at him guardedly.

'Because I'd seen you on a local chat show just a week before, and I was so knocked out by that flagrant sex appeal of yours, sweetheart, that all I could think about was how I could get to meet you.' Surprised by his frank admission, she felt a warm surge of colour creeping up her throat. 'When you wrote to Alec asking for an interview, I seized the opportunity—and coincidence,' he inserted with a grimace, 'with both hands. You see, you're here because *I* wanted you here, Lee.'

His soft arrogance had her taking a step back, one hand clutching the towel around her. 'You mean. . .' She hesitated, trying to get to grips with what he was saying. 'You mean that at that party the other night. . .you knew who I was? That I was Lee Roman?' she amended, as aghast as if he had just discovered her real identity.

His smile acknowledged it.

'And you didn't tell me who *you* were. . .' Heat scorched her cheeks as her voice tailed off, the silence broken only by the hum of summer insects. 'You bastard,' she whispered, sweeping away from him. She gave a small cry as he caught her wrist, his fingers cruel on her soft flesh, forcing her to face him.

'And what's the female equivalent?' His face had hardened in uncompromising lines, and the deep chest expanded heavily. 'You were playing some warped little game of your own, remember?' he accused with a quiet anger, his eyes darkening beneath the enviably thick fringes of his lashes. 'I wanted to tell you immediately, but I thought you'd be dubious about getting

involved with the relative of someone you'd come here
to work with—but I would have come clean before the
evening was through. When you adopted a complete
change of attitude, however, I decided a little surprise
wouldn't do you any harm at all.'

'Thanks!' said Lee, brittly, trying to extricate herself
from him and failing miserably, gaining no comfort
either from the thought that, had she been in his
position the other night, she would most probably have
done the same thing. But that she was here only
through *his* instigation made her feel oddly panicky—
as if she was losing control over her own life—so that,
totally discomfited, she was throwing back at him,
'And how was I supposed to repay you for
your. . .generosity? By jumping into your bed?'

'Well. . .' The mocking curve to that firm mouth
made her instantly regret her imprudent remark. 'I
wasn't expecting anything so. . .magnanimous, but
since you made the suggestion. . .'

Her eyes widening with shocked anger, she was too
taken aback to drag away the hand he was lifting to his
lips, and she caught her breath as he dipped his head
to the small, throbbing pulse in her wrist, his tongue
playing gently across the skin his tenacious grip had
bruised, so warm and so sensual that a sudden, traitorous excitement leaped through her.

'You really are the most. . .' Suddenly she found the
strength to wrench her hand away, alarmed by the
shaming intensity of her own response. Breathless, her
nostrils flaring, she grasped at the towel that would
have slid from her shoulders, pulling it around her like
a protective armour against him. 'Are you always so
persistent with a woman who clearly isn't interested?'

'No.' His very positive reply brought her head up to
meet the disturbing penetration of his eyes. 'But you

protest too much, Lee,' he commented softly, his finger tracing the gentle outline of her cheek. 'And *that* intrigues me. . .'

She took a swift, sharp breath, not sure whether it was the brush of his hand against her lips or that hard, calculating shrewdness that had her suddenly tensing, her heart hammering crazily in her breast. The buzz of a speedboat intruded upon her senses, somewhere out at sea, beyond the reefs. . .and then, closer to hand, a voice, feminine and distantly familiar, which had Lee's blood coagulating in her veins.

CHAPTER FOUR

'JORDAN! Jordan, darling! Are you out here?' They both turned as the tall redhead approached, Lee desperately wishing she could run away and hide. 'Alec told me you were entertaining some journalist. . .'

Her words tailed off as she looked condescendingly at Lee, her eyes narrowing beneath brows that were the same sorrel as the short, well-layered hair, and Lee's heart seemed to stop. As a constant visitor to his house, Richard's personal assistant—unlike Jordan—had known her too well to have forgotten her, surely? Lee thought, with her blood curdling, waiting tensely to be ruthlessly exposed at any second. But there was no instant recognition in Madeline Eastman's lovely face; just a cold, pointed, feminine suspicion, Lee noted curiously, with a sigh of relief, and as Jordan made the introductions Lee realised why.

So this was the secretary Arlene had mentioned. The woman he was 'nicely tied up with' in New York!

She had forgotten though, how tall Madeline was— almost as tall as Jordan— a figure-hugging green suit adding a mature elegance to her slim figure as she looked down at Lee and uttered on a small, awed note, 'You're *the* Lee Roman. . .of *Eve's*!'

Queasily, Lee nodded, wondering if the woman would still be so impressed if she knew the state the magazine was in.

'I didn't know you were a fan of the journal, Madeline?' Beside them, Jordan sounded faintly amused, his voice as smooth as velvet after the American woman's rather jarring tones.

'Oh, you know me, darling. I'll read anything when I'm bored enough.' She sent a sultry smile up into those very masculine features which, curiously, was not returned with the same besotted indulgence.

'That was hardly called for, Madeline.' It took Lee a moment to realise that he was practically defending her magazine, when yesterday he'd been totally detrimental about it himself. But then, he'd been angry, she reflected, warm colour washing up over her skin from the memory of that punishing kiss in her bedroom.

'Oh, come on, darling!' Through her disquieting reverie, she heard the woman's embarrassed little laugh. 'You know I didn't mean it like *that*!'

But she did, Lee thought—exactly like that, remembering how spiteful Madeline could be from past experience.

Absently, she heard the wind shiver through the poinciana tree, and pulled the towel more closely around her, noticing the small bank of cloud that had drifted in from the sea.

'Well, since you're here. . .are you going to join us in a swim?' Jordan suggested more amiably, and, glancing up at the clouds above the grand structure of the house, added wryly, 'Before it rains.'

'You must be joking!' Madeline followed his glance skywards, pulling a face, her flawless beauty not so vibrant as it had once been, Lee noted, realising that the woman had to be over thirty now. 'Isn't it just typical. . .' she was adding to no one in particular '. . .how I always get the lousiest of weather the instant I step off a plane? Anyway, Jordan. . .' she sent a dubious glance in Lee's direction '. . .I wouldn't like to be accused of interrupting anything.'

'Don't worry, you won't be,' said Lee, deciding to
go in, because with her damp hair and nothing but a
wet, see-through bikini under the towel she was beginning to feel like a wilting daisy beside Madeline
Eastman. Also, in her bare feet she was considerably
shorter than Madeline, and, caught as she was between
her and Jordan's imposing stature, she was reminded
too much of the vulnerable adolescent Madeline had
thrown on his mercy before. Involuntarily, she
shuddered.

'Where are you going?' It was a hard demand from
Jordan as Lee began moving away, the sudden, puzzling question in the other woman's eyes causing her
skin to heat.

'I have to telephone my office,' she said, which was
the truth, even if she was using it as an excuse to get
away. But that confounded tremor in her voice hadn't
escaped him, she realised, if that thin line between his
eyes was anything to go by. However, he said nothing,
merely dipping his head in acquiescence, so that Lee
tore herself away, wondering how long this whole
ridiculous state of affairs could last.

Physical appearances might change, but other char-
acteristics didn't, she thought, tripping across the patio.
And Madeline had known her well. Therefore, there
was every chance that, sooner or later, it would dawn
upon the woman who she was. Not only that, she hated
this feeling of guilt, particularly where Alec was concerned, and yet if she decided to abandon her feature
she wouldn't only be unable to give him a reason, but
would have wasted his time and her own—Vince's
too—and the *Apple* was far from sound enough to
suffer the expense of a futile assignment.

Despairingly, she went indoors, feeling the air-con-
ditioning like a cool douche on her skin after the sub-
tropical heat outside. There was no sign of Alec or

Arlene, for which she was glad. She didn't think she could have faced seeing anyone else just then, and presumed that the therapist would already have left, while Alec would be resting in his room.

In her own, Lee showered and dressed, deciding there was nothing she could do but carry on as if Madeline hadn't arrived. She had more than herself to consider, after all. But as she applied a scarlet lipstick to blend with a predominantly red sun-dress, she reflected on how long Madeline must have been working for Jordan. Probably ever since his father had died, she assumed, because she recalled him making the woman an offer at the time. And feeling cowardly all of a sudden, as she finished finger-drying her hair, she rang Vince at the hotel, and was relieved when he not only answered his phone, but was free to meet her for lunch.

'How are you finding Bermuda?' she asked, when she was sitting opposite him in the Tudor-style restaurant, glad she had brought a raincoat because the rain Jordan had forecast was coming down in a torrent now, making itself evident in little rivulets on the diamond-paned windows.

Vince dragged his gaze reluctantly away from a buxom waitress, dressed as a serving wench, and pulled a satisfied grin. 'Curvy. How about you?'

With a groan, Lee rolled her eyes, toying with a seafood casserole. She should have expected no less from Vince, she realised, her eyes drawn to the rather ostentatious gold ingot in the open V of his shirt. But she decided to tell him, desperate for a friend to unburden her heart upon. She'd always been too busy to have any close friends—of either gender—and oddly enough, she realised now, Vince was about the closest. So she told him how she'd made a fool of herself with

Jordan the other night, and how he'd turned up at Mason's the following day, adding, as she studied a succulent-looking prawn which she suddenly seemed to have lost all appetite for, 'He treated me badly in the past and I wanted to get my own back, but it all went wrong.'

'So that's why I was supposed to come up and rescue you.' Vince sent her an apologetic look. 'Sorry, ol' love. I'd have been there on the dot if I'd known. What a man to try and mess around with, though!' His soft whistle through his teeth didn't help to appease her in any way. She knew how stupid she'd been! And suddenly, over the clink of crockery, the drone of conversation, Vince was leaning across the rustic table to ask in lowered, rather awed tones, 'Was he your lover?'

She didn't know why that question should bring the colour rushing to her cheeks—make her heart beat faster—but it did, and quickly she popped the prawn into her mouth in a deliberate attempt to keep her head averted so that Vince wouldn't see.

'No,' she said, forcing herself to swallow, though the food seemed to be sticking in her throat. 'He thought his father had had that privilege.'

Vince's blue eyes widened. 'What. . .that you and his father were——' He broke off, clearly shocked. Then, to her astonishment, he asked, 'Were you?'

'No, I was not!' she snapped back, although when he pretended to be jerked back on to his seat from a mock right-hand blow, almost knocking a cup out of someone's hand, she couldn't repress a giggle. He was only being naturally inquisitive, after all. But she was a very private person, and, though Vince knew a lot about her, he didn't know she had lived with Richard, or about the money the man had left her, and she decided not to enlighten him now. She had never been able to explain the man's generosity, and it had aroused too much speculation about her as it was.

The storm had abated by the time they left the restaurant, and the wet tarmac glistened under a sun that shone as vividly as if it had never stopped. Vince had hired a moped and offered her a lift back, and Lee's first concern about not being properly protected to ride pillion was dispelled when he miraculously produced two helmets.

'I might have guessed!' she grinned, slipping one on as she sat behind him astride the bike. Where the prospect of female company was concerned, Vince was always prepared. 'Who's the lucky girl today?'

'Why, Lee!' He angled towards her, a look of mock affrontry sobering his rakish features, a hand across his heart. 'You know there's only one for me. She buys me lunch and makes no demands upon me whatsoever. And that's the trouble.' He gave a teasing grimace before turning away to start the ignition. 'Unfortunately, all I am to her is a tax-deductable expense!'

Lee gave him a friendly prod as he put the bike into motion, and felt her spirits lifting as they soared down the hill, along the damp, leafy lanes. The wind was refreshing in her face as she looked towards the rolling terrain of one of the island's many golf-courses, almost envying the leisurely figures ambling across its verdant slopes. The sea stretched beyond it, sparkling blue, while closer to hand the colour-washed walls of the island houses made a quaint picture under the mid-May sun. Pinks stood beside soft yellows and pastel blues like cubes of colourful candy, each one topped with the same conventional white roof, designed, she remembered Alec telling her that morning, to trap the rain—the island's main source of fresh water—which was then channelled through gutters and stored in tanks below the ground. And whether it was the effect of the wine she had been drinking with so little to eat in comparison, or a release of the tension she'd felt for the first time since meeting Jordan again, she wasn't sure, but suddenly she was laughing aloud, inciting Vince to glance over his shoulder and shout above the noise of the engine, 'That's better! You looked like the pits when we started lunch.'

So he noticed, she thought, surprised, even if he *had* been eyeing the waitresses! She couldn't resist giving the waist to which she was clinging an affectionate little squeeze, grateful that she could always rely on Vince to cheer her up.

She should have remembered, too, that she could always rely upon him to deliberately misinterpret any gesture of affection on her part—however small— because as soon as she stepped off the bike, shaking her hair free of the confining helmet, his arm suddenly snaked around her.

'Does this mean you've changed your mind about me?' he teased, kissing her before she even realised what was happening. She had to use both hands to extricate herself from his bearlike hug.

'No, it doesn't!' she assured him adamantly, although his face was so alive with mischief that it was difficult injecting enough authority into her voice to add, 'Kindly remember, Vince Harris, that I am still your boss.'

She thought she heard him laughing as he accelerated away, and still wearing her mask of mock severity she turned and walked straight into Jordan.

He smiled at her startled gasp, one strong, steadying hand at her elbow. 'Well,' he drawled, amused, his eyes taking in the colour she could feel stealing traitor-ously across her skin. 'You certainly told him, didn't you?' He was wearing a light tailored shirt and a pair of snug-fitting cream trousers, and Lee couldn't speak for a moment, finding that casual elegance of his quite breathtaking after Vince's rather garish taste, this unexpected contact with him a complete assault upon her senses. 'What did he do, little Eve. . .sample the forbidden fruit?'

Something other than mockery had her pulling away from him in fear, but fear of something that was emotive and wholly sensual, and which had nothing to do with the past.

'Do you usually get your kicks out of eavesdrop-ping?' she threw at him, struggling for equanimity. And, without waiting for an answer, she turned to go inside.

A swift movement of gravel, and he had caught up, falling into step beside her. 'I could hardly help it!' he stated drily. 'The man wasn't being particularly discreet.'

And you would be, she supplied silently, for no reason, and was shocked at the spontaneous imagery such thoughts of him gave rise to. Inevitably, that fine vein of tension threaded its way through her body, and she kept her gaze glued to the ground and her red-sandalled feet, so that he wouldn't realise how uneasy she was just being with him.

'I've managed to talk Alec into getting out this afternoon.' With superlative courtesy he stood back to let her precede him into the house. 'He needs a change of scenery, and we thought it would be a good idea to incorporate some photos, too, while he's out. So you'd better ring your. . .' his lips twisted derisively

'. . .Romeo, as soon as he gets back to the hotel, and arrange for him to meet you both.'

Lee nodded, catching the fragrance of some cut flowers which stood in a large vase on the hall-table, their sweet, evocative scent lingering with the pleasant aroma of freshly ground coffee. 'And Vince isn't my Romeo,' she retorted tartly, annoyed by the derogatory way in which Jordan had described the photographer. 'He's a friend.'

'And friendship holds no complications?'

They had reached the foot of the wide cedar staircase that was a feature of the house, and Lee drew up sharply as, with a smooth spontaneity, Jordan brought his arm across the carved banister, barring her way.

'I don't know what you mean,' she parried, trying to keep her voice level—her face composed beneath his cool, discerning scrutiny—because she knew very well. She clutched her rolled-up raincoat and bag to her breasts as if her life depended upon them. 'Would you let me pass, please?'

Surprisingly, he let his hand fall, but before she could move he said matter-of-factly, 'You weren't at lunch.'

Those dark eyes scanned the tense, delicate symmetry of her features, his so acutely masculine beneath that thick black hair that she caught her breath. Why, in heaven's name should this man in particular hold such a vibrant attraction for her? she wondered, sick at herself, because, dear lord, he did. But, sticking out her chin, she said as dispassionately as she could, 'I didn't realise I'd be missed. Anyway, I thought you'd appreciate some time alone with M. . .your secretary,' she thought to amend quickly, 'especially as she seemed rather put out earlier, finding another woman swimming with her boss.'

She pushed past him then, trying to ignore that pleasant scent of him that made her want to inhale more deeply—the shock, like something electric, that ran through her when her hand had accidentally brushed his.

Behind her she heard him say, 'Madeline's here to fulfil duties—which she does very well, incidentally—with very little claim upon my private life. And yes. . .you were missed at lunch.'

Abusrdly, the soft delivery of that last comment made her heart skip a beat, her brain cogitating over what he had said about Madeline's limited claims to him. Did that mean that he wasn't as serious about his secretary as Arlene had led her to believe? Anyway, what did *she* care? she endeavoured to convince herself, turning on the bottom stair, her hand tightening on the banister when she realised that those few inches had brought her to meet his height, and that his eyes were disturbingly level with hers. Totally dismantled, she gave a shrug and, with an awkward little smile, uttered, 'Sorry. . .a natural mistake. Although I suppose she's bound to be a bit possessive of you after so long.'

Even before those thick brows knitted, she realised her blunder. Mortified by her own stupidity, she saw him looking at her askance.

'How do you know how long it's been?'

Of course. No one had told her. How could she have been so lax?

'Alec mentioned it,' she lied, her brain working quickly. And, just in case Jordan checked with his uncle and discovered that it wasn't true, she added, 'I think.' After all, it could always have been Arlene, she thought, in an attempt to reassure herself. Or one of the servants. 'I'll go and ring Vince.'

She almost ran up the stairs away from him, and was virtually at the top when she heard his deep, authoritative voice below. 'Isn't there something of vital importance which you seem to have overlooked?'

Lee froze in her tracks, touching her tongue to her top lip as she turned round and saw the hard, heart-stopping question in his eyes. He knows, she thought, horrified. Madeline must have told him!

'W-what?' She exhaled, her heart beating so fast now that she felt dizzy, her nails digging into suddenly clammy palms.

'The venue for Vince,' he said phlegmatically, coming upstairs with that self-assured air that made Lee want to hit him. 'You can hardly expect him to meet you if he doesn't know where you're likely to be, can you?'

Which made sense, Lee thought, hoping her relief wasn't too apparent, although she could have kicked herself for not thinking of it herself.

Glad to be getting out of the house—away from him for a few hours—she soon realised how premature her gratitude was, when she tripped light-heartedly out to Alec's sedate saloon a little later and saw Jordan sitting in the driver's seat. Her heart sank. She'd automatically assumed Matthew would be driving.

'Could I sit in the back?' she requested with a small crack in her voice when he got out and opened the front passenger door for her.

An eyebrow lifted, although he said nothing, opening the door at the rear. But as she stooped to get in beside his uncle he bent unsettlingly close to her and said quietly enough so that Alec wouldn't hear, 'Carry on like this, darling, and you'll wind up breaking his heart.'

His totally blatant intimation that she was currying

favour with his uncle infuriated her, but she ignored it, flashing him a smile that was entirely forced as he closed her door. She simply felt for Alec, that was all. Being relegated to the status of back-seat passenger in one's own car couldn't be much fun for anyone, and the man seemed more than delighted that she'd decided to join him there.

Meeting that dark gaze in the mirror, though, that made her instantly look away, rather guiltily she had to admit that it was her own disturbing reaction to Jordan, as much as any consideration for his uncle, that had steered her away from sharing the intimate confines of the front seat with him.

They met Vince near the Gibb's Hill lighthouse, an impressive white pinnacle overlooking the Great Sound, and not far from the restaurant where they had had lunch.

Suggesting a spot that would take in Bermuda's famous landmark, Lee was surprised at how skilfully Jordan handled his uncle, getting him out of the car and into his chair with none of the difficulty she and Arlene had experienced that morning.

'I'll want a seaward profile, Vince. Get those dinghies in if you can,' Lee was instructing as soon as they were ready to start, pointing to some brightly coloured craft on the blue water in the distance. 'And I'll need some close-ups, too. Full frame. Head and shoulders. . .' She threw herself into her work with her usual enthusiasm, while Jordan stood leaning against a tree with his arms folded, an amused curl to his lips.

With Vince capably following her instructions, Lee stuffed her hands into the pockets of the slacks she'd substituted for her sun-dress, and moved up the gentle hillside to get a closer view of the lighthouse.

'If you want to get up there, you'll have to climb

something not far short of two hundred steps.' She
swung round to see Jordan behind her, and she tensed,
then smiled uneasily. 'Make sure it's a day when it isn't
windy, though,' he went on to advise drily. 'It's safe
enough, but it does have a reputation for swaying.'

'You're kidding?' she looked at him, eyes widening
in astonishment, then burst out laughing when she
realised he was in deadly earnest.

'You should do that more often. It suits you,' he said
quietly.

Lee caught her breath, reluctant to acknowledge the
sudden warm surge in her blood, and, needing a
diversion, gave all her attention to the lighthouse.
There were people way up there on the balcony now,
looking out over the Sound and Hamilton, and the vast
stretch of open ocean beyond. Unaccountably, she
gave a little shudder.

And, of course, he noticed.

'Don't you have a head for heights, little Eve?'

Against the whispering of the waves and the continuous clicking of Vince's camera a little way off,
Jordan's voice was seductively soft. There was sensual-
ity, too, in his use of the nickname he'd chosen to give
her, and, disconcerted, Lee pressed her lips together,
before returning stiffly, 'I just happen to like both feet
planted firmly on solid ground.'

Reluctant to be alone with him, she started back
down the slope.

'Actually, the view up there's quite spectacular,'
Jordan was enlarging, ignoring the snub and walking
with her, the strong lines and curves of his face
strikingly handsome as she stole a glance at him almost
against her will. 'If you come at the right time of year,
of course, sometimes it's possible to get a glimpse of
the whales migrating. . .' his chin jerked seawards.

'. . .out beyond the reefs, and that's some sight. One of nature's splendours. Dark, graceful and magnificent.'

The appreciation in the deep voice had her meeting his gaze with some surprise. Of course, he would have a great respect for nature—for life—she was startled to recognise, then pushed the absurd notion aside. She hardly knew him. How could she know that? Nevertheless, the thought of those superb mammals actually swimming out there in that translucent blue water did funny things to her stomach, and she found herself responding rather more amiably, 'Now, that's something you would get me up there to see!'

'You can tell she's a city girl, can't you, Jordan?' The older man had overheard and was glancing their way, those autocratic features amused, clearly mistaking the reason for the flush in Lee's cheeks. 'A bit different from New York here, isn't it?' he commented. 'Although I'd take a guess you weren't actually raised there, were you?'

Lee gulped, her eyes trained on Vince, who was on his haunches, fixing a lens to his camera. Uncomfortably, she felt Jordan's interest—hard and intent—that dark gaze perceptive of every change of mood, every small fear.

'Are you thinking what I am, Alec?' His eyes never left her face. 'That the lady has a rather intriguing accent? It's soft, unobstrusive and *very* sexy, but a product of the "Big Apple", definitely not. Where's your real home, Lee?'

Her stomach churning, quickly she darted a glance at Vince, hoping he wouldn't say anthing that would unintentionally give her away. One hint that she was English and Jordan might well put two and two together, and if he did she could kiss goodbye to her feature on Alec right now. She should have warned Vince, she realised, rather belatedly.

Fortunately, though, the photographer was still preoccupied with his camera, and so, picking her words carefully, Lee replied, 'New York's been my home for as long as I care to remember. If my accent's a bit mixed, it's probably because my parents moved around a lot when I was a child,' she added evasively, remembering her mother's continual dissatisfaction, her constant yearning for a bigger house, a better neighbourhood.

'OK, guv! Just a couple more. Left profile, I think. . .'

Vince was back in action, recapturing his subject with that professionalism she'd admired about him from the day he'd first walked into her office, and for a few moments she watched, appreciating his skill.

'Alec mentioned that you lost your father.' The rich, tonal quality of Jordan's voice was more striking than usual after the younger man's broad Cockney, and Lee cast a tentative tongue over her lips, finding herself back on a one-to-one basis with him again. So he'd been discussing her with his uncle. She nodded.

'What about your mother?' He rested his hand against the smooth bark of a young tree, his voice soft, almost coaxing, against the distant wash of the ocean.

'My father was separated from my mother.' She lifted a slim shoulder beneath her thin blouse. 'I don't see her.'

A tiny crease brought the black brows together. 'Oh?' Obviously he thought it unusual.

'It was the way she wanted it,' she said, without elucidating further.

'I'm sorry.'

Was that sympathy—or almost pained understanding

flickering in the dark depths of his eyes? she wondered curiously. Had he sensed the regret in her? Because, oddly, it still hurt. Perhaps she had been part of the drudgery her mother had given up for her freedom, probably thinking that at sixteen her daughter hadn't needed her any more. But she had!

'It's OK,' she said, deciding she had imagined that sensitivity in him, because it had gone now. 'It was a long time ago.' And with a swish of dark hair she turned and swept away from him, glad that Vince had finished the session and was packing up his equipment, because the last person she wanted to get emotional with was Jordan Colyer.

Dinner was a test of endurance, a meal during which Madeline Eastman monopolised Jordan's attentions with a lack of subtlety Lee found painful to watch. Madeline was besotted with her employer, she thought, feeling almost sorry for her in view of the weary indulgence with which Jordan responded.

'I'm having a few business associates in for dinner on Saturday night,' Alec was saying, swirling a rich claret around his glass, 'and I'd deem it an honour if you would consider acting as hostess for me, Lee.' He laughed at the surprise on her face. 'I find these things tedious,' he went on to enlighten her, his weary expression confirming it. 'It's also a confounded nuisance being patronised by a lot of condescending customers who like to think I've lost my wits as well as my ability to walk. With a pretty woman beside me, though, it just might show them that there's still some life in the old dog yet.'

From across the table she felt Jordan's dark and inscrutable interest, while there was a tense whiteness about Madeline's lovely face that couldn't conceal her silent anger at not being asked.

'All you have to do is charm a lot of stuffy old men,' she uttered, as though the whole thing was beneath her, and she gave Lee one of those uncomfortably searching looks that had had her on tenterhooks all evening, wondering if the woman had suddenly guessed who she was.

It must be hard on Alec, though, trying to maintain status with his more able-bodied associates, Lee thought, feeling for him, and with an understanding smile she said gently, 'I'd be very happy to,' wondering at the sceptical eyebrow Jordan raised as she glanced briefly in his direction.

It was a relief when the meal was over, and she spent the next hour or so in her room, typing out the notes for her feature. Then, deciding on an early night, she showered, pulled on an apricot silk nightdress and, finding the thick paperback book she'd bought at the airport to read on the plane, climbed into bed.

She must have fallen asleep, because the next thing she knew she was lying in the lamplight feeling decidedly chilly, and she started as a dull thud came from the room directly beneath hers. Then another. In sudden alarm, she remembered that it was Alec's bedroom immediately below, unable as he was to use the stairs, and a glance at her discarded watch showed that it was already after twelve.

Without another thought she scrambled out of bed and down the stairs, finding the study door open, but pausing for a second—her heart in her mouth—before tapping tentatively on the door to the room beyond.

A groan, hardly as audible as her thudding heartbeat, reached her, and in panic she threw open the door, a small cry leaving her lips at the alarming sight that met her.

CHAPTER FIVE

ALEC was half-lying on the carpeted floor, his face flushed from the effort of trying to haul himself up between the wardrobe and the chest of drawers.

'What the. . .?' Lee's hand flew to her throat, the colour draining out of her cheeks as she saw the pained look on his face, heard his feeble supplication.

'For goodness' sake, Lee! Help me.'

She didn't need to be asked twice. Darting across the room, she offered her assistance immediately, although she wasn't strong enough to help him up by herself. After a few vain attempts she said hopelessly, 'It's no good. I'd better get Jordan.'

'No!' He grabbed her hand as she made to move away. 'He's gone out with Madeline.' His breathing was hard and laborious. 'No. . .' He gestured towards his chair just a few feet away. 'I'll be able to ease myself up if you could just bring it closer.'

Quickly, Lee did as requested, positioning it as near to him as she possibly could, and by allowing him to lever himself up with the help of her shoulder she managed to get him back into the wheelchair, though she winced silently once or twice from the weight which was rather too much for her slender frame.

Not until he had wheeled himself over to the bed and was easing himself on to it did she ask, 'How did you wind up on the floor, anyway?' Absently, she noted that he had his pyjamas on under the red-quilted dressing-gown.

'I wanted a handkerchief, that's all,' he informed

her, exasperated, his chest rising heavily under the gold
edging of his gown. 'I wanted to get it myself, without
being totally dependent on anybody else for a change.'
He grimaced up at her rather anxious face, his silver
hair tinged pink from the bedside-lamp. 'And I don't
want anyone else knowing about this,' he forewarned
her, an unwitting reminder of how sensitive he was
about his helplessness. 'A pity you had to come in and
find me like that. I can't do a blasted thing on my own.'

'And you shouldn't have!' Lee wailed in protest,
fetching him a handkerchief from the drawer he had
been trying to open, although, in a way, she understood
that indomitable pride. Hadn't she always been determined to cope alone? She realised now that it was
Jordan, with his cruel, barbed words eight years ago—
as well as her mother—who had helped create that
hard resolve for independence in her. 'You could have
caused yourself a terrible injury.' She stepped back,
looking down at Alec with her hair falling wildly about
her face, her eyes filled with reprimanding concern.
'Trying something like that on your own was no less
than stubborn.'

As soon as she had said it, she bit her tongue,
wondering if she'd taken too much of a liberty. She
hardly knew the man, after all! But almost good-
naturedly, he grumbled, still breathless, 'You're beginning to sound like Arlene,' so that, for his own sake,
Lee decided to press the point.

'Well, she's right,' she sided, and, more worried
about him than she liked to admit, asked, 'Are you all
right? Don't you think I should send for the doctor?'

'You'll do nothing of the kind!' His brusque rejoinder split the stillness of the room—made her start—
and with a weary smile he said more gently, 'Don't
fuss. Jordan's taking me for my routine check-up in the

morning, anyway.' With some effort he reached down to pull the folded duvet up over his legs. 'You told Arlene you nursed your father before he died,' he reminded Lee as she moved to help him. 'He was a lucky man having a daughter like you.' He gave her a speculative smile when he saw her modest blush. 'Were you as bossy with him?'

'Sometimes,' she murmured, with a lump in her throat—a ridiculous welling of nostalgia. And through the sudden ache of loneliness inside her she heard Alec recommend softly, 'Come and sit down. Here.' He patted the edge of the bed beside him. 'Tell me about him.'

So she did. From the man's unerring patience and kindness, to that last holiday they had had together before he'd had his heart attack, until, a long time later, hearing Alec's deep, steady breathing, she realised he had fallen asleep.

She stood up, drawing the duvet around him and extinguishing his lamp, letting her eyes adjust to the darkness, when a beam of light streaked across the curtains. Jordan! His car was so finely tuned, she hadn't heard it come in, but now she was aware of it purring to a halt outside the window, of the handbrake being applied.

She moved out into the study, and, totally averse to meeting either he or Madeline at this time of night, waited there in the shadows as the hall light was snapped on, the sound of the woman's high heels echoing across the hall with her little peals of laughter, accompanied by the occasional intervention of Jordan's deep, laconic tones. Then their voices died away.

The thought of the two of them in some cosy clinch in the drawing-room intruded on her consciousness, but she shook it aside, peeping around the door. All was quiet now, and she ventured out into the hall, glancing over her shoulder like some fugitive before pulling the study door after her—and gasped with shock when she turned to see Jordan standing there, staring down at her.

'Alec. . .is he all right?' Concern was evident in the deep groove between his brows, and Lee nodded, swallowing. Gracious! Why had she to bump into him?

'He's fine.' She didn't know what else to say, suddenly very conscious of the fact that in her haste to get downstairs earlier she hadn't bothered to put anything over her nightdress, while Jordan was impeccably dressed in a silver-grey suit, white shirt and silver tie. 'In fact, he's asleep,' she thought to add quickly, to allay any further fears Jordan might have, which she realised was the wrong thing to say when his frown deepened, and he moved closer.

'Then what were you doing in there?'

He was so close that she couldn't think straight, and she shifted her weight uncomfortably from one foot to the other, her face pale against the dark halo of her hair. 'I—I. . .' Heard a noise, she was about to say, then stopped herself in time. Alec had almost implored her not to tell anyone, and if she told Jordan what had brought her down here she could find herself breaking Alec's trust. So, rather hesitantly, she uttered. 'I just thought I'd pop in and see if he was all right, that's all.'

Something leaped in his eyes. 'What. . .dressed like that?' One doubting glance ran over her flimsy attire, then directed itself at the wall clock at the far end of the hall. 'At a quarter to one in the morning?' he finished on a note of pure incredulity.

What was in his mind was obvious, and, unconsciously, Lee clutched the lace edges of her nightdress just above her breasts, anger stirring in her.

'Just what are you implying?' she demanded, eyes narrowing, a faint hint of colour stealing across her cheeks.

'I'm not implying anything,' he returned, one hand pushing back the fine quality jacket. 'Just making an observation.'

'Then keep your observations to yourself!'

Her chin in the air, she made to flounce away from him, and was brought up sharply by the arm which lifted to the panelled wall with almost insulting casualness in front of her.

'My, my! We've got a pretty quick temper, haven't we?' Caught in the aura of that devastating masculinity, she felt her mouth go dry. The propinquity of his long-limbed body sent tongues of awareness licking through her, her faltering gaze, not daring to challenge his, lingering for eternal seconds on the hard leanness of his waist. But his near-accusation stung—a nettle-edged reminder of his verbal brutality when she had been too young to defend herself—and she met the uncompromising strength of his features to taunt with daring intrepidity, 'So what are *we* going to do—curb it?'

Something like hard puzzlement etched deep grooves around his eyes and mouth, that ominous glitter in the dark irises warning her that she was being utterly foolish in her constant need to lash out at him, and just for a moment made her actually fear some sort of physical retaliation. But his mouth was twisting in a parody of a smile, and he said with soft, almost alarming control, 'If I ever put you where you belong, Lee, I'll not only curb that temper, I'll——'

Madeline's sudden querying call cut him short, and Lee saw him tense beneath the immaculate suit. Flushed from sparring with him, she faced him with a rebellious thrust to her bottom lip, angry fire in her eyes, although the chilling contempt in the gaze that tugged down over her clinging nightdress actually caused her to shiver.

'I suggest you take *temptation* out of my way, little Eve,' he breathed with cutting emphasis, 'and go back to bed before you catch your death of cold.'

She didn't wait to be told again, grateful for her chance to get away from him.

When she came downstairs the following morning, the front door was open. Sunlight was streaming in and she could see Alec already outside, sitting in the car. Jordan was speaking to Matthew in the hall, when he suddenly looked up and saw her, his swift, assessing glance over her white sleeveless top and jeans sending an odd tingle through her.

'I'm taking Alec for his check-up,' he told her as the Bermudian moved away. 'We should be a couple of hours. You could come with us, if you fancy a drive.'

She would have liked to have said 'yes', if only to see some more of the country, but the thought of spending time alone with Jordan while his uncle was with the doctor wasn't something she relished. So she said, casually, 'Thanks, but I think I'll stay here.' And she guessed, from the sudden darkening of his eyes, that he obviously thought she considered sitting around hospital waiting-rooms beneath her.

Well, let him think what he liked! she thought exasperatedly, still smarting from his unjust intimations the previous night.

Watching him stride away from her, though, she couldn't help experiencing a reluctant tug of respect for him. That he was spending what little free time he had catering for his uncle's needs, when he could so easily have let the staff do it, said a lot for the man's character—made her suddenly despair of his all too apparent conclusions about her just now. And, finding herself with no appetite for breakfast, she took herself back upstairs to add several more paragraphs to her story, made contact with her office, and then, keen to avoid Madeline, decided to take a leisurely bus journey and spend the morning in Hamilton.

When she returned shortly before lunch she had invested in one or two souvenirs, a bottle of perfume for Rachael, a bird-feeder to hang on her balcony back home, and a new dress for the dinner-party the following night.

Jordan came out of his uncle's study just as she was crossing the hall, and he pulled a wry face at all the parcels she was carrying.

'Why didn't you tell me you were going into Hamilton?' he reprimanded softly as he approached, obviously quick to notice the name on one of the bags. 'Didn't you realise we were going there?' With amazing reflexes he caught one of the parcels that was slipping from her grasp, placing it on top of the rest. 'Or does this display of total independence mean you'd rather manage without demeaning yourself to ask my help?'

Instantly, Lee's hackles rose, his sudden antagonism with those dangerous sensations his nearness stirred in her unavoidably fuelling her own.

'Whatever I said, you'd take it as a direct insult against you,' she spat, finding this continual conflict with him extremely wearing.

'Try me.'

His hard suggestion made her hesitate, something about the taut planes and angles of his face almost inviting her to respond to him. It would have been easy then to explain that it had been a spur of the moment thing—that she hadn't known she'd be going out herself until after he'd left. But there could be no fraternising with him, she warned herself, not least because a small, weak part of her suddenly wanted to. So, choosing to ignore his last comment, she asked with genuine solicitude, 'More importantly, how did it go with Alec?'

There was a transient darkening of his eyes, as if he were considering the reason for her query, before he said simply, 'Fine. His blood pressure's up a bit, but the doctor seems to think that if he keeps up this rate of progress, he could well be walking again within six months.'

She could sense an unexpressed relief in him, so great she could almost touch it, and for a moment they measured glances, without hostility, just two people linked in mutual concern. A silent communication that seemed to send odd vibrations through her, giving rise to the ridiculous notion suddenly that she *knew* this man—had known him all her life—a feeling so intense and uncanny that it took her breath away, filled her with an almost incalculable regret that things couldn't have been different. . .

Tremulously, she murmured, 'I'm glad,' and tore away from him before he could guess at the very disconcerting feelings inside of her.

Dinner the following evening was attended by a dozen or so of Alec's contemporaries and their wives, and, despite his earlier admission to hating such affairs, the man positively shone. Arlene, who had come in briefly that afternoon for a progress report rather than to administer any therapy, had commented that she'd never known him so easy to get along with. Then she startled Lee by adding, 'I think it's because you're here. You seem to have a humanising effect on him!'

It wouldn't have been so embarrassing, Lee thought now, sipping champagne on the romantically lit patio, if Jordan hadn't come out of the house at that moment and overheard. He hadn't made any comment, though; he'd simply plunged into the pool. And though she herself had laughed aside Arlene's remark as fanciful, silently she had to admit to a growing rapport between herself and the industrialist not entirely unlike that which she had shared with her own father.

'. . .you know, Jordan, we really must thank you for what you did for Barry. The boy's really serious about his career now, after that pep talk you gave him last time you were here. I don't know. . .Giles and I couldn't make him see sense, but *you*. . .well, he seemed to listen to you. . .'

Outside the small group in which Lee was standing, the enthusiastic female voice impinged on the warm night air. Reluctantly, though, Lee felt a wave of acknowledgment ripple through her. Jordan Colyer was very much the type of man mothers would want to influence their sons—the type that younger men might even try to emulate, she surprised herself by thinking, as she heard his unembarrassed response.

Aware that she was listening to every intonation, every inflexion in that deep voice—that her senses were too finely tuned to the man—she began to feel like Madeline, who was clinging possessively to his arm, hanging on to his every word, and surreptitiously Lee moved out of his disturbing sphere to give her full attention to something his uncle was saying.

'So where did you find her, Alec?'

'You're a dark old rascal, keeping a prize like that from the rest of us.'

'Where have you been hiding her these past few months?'

They were talking about her, teasing remarks that were bandied around the little group of elderly men as after-dinner discussions were diluted with more and more brandy, and Lee humoured them for Alec's sake, knowing he was enjoying his colleagues' mistaken conclusions.

Conscious that someone had come up behind her, obviously lured by the jollity of the little group, Lee moved to allow the newcomer into the small circle, taking the opportunity to slip away for a few moments to herself.

'Walking away from me again, little Eve?' Jordan's features were mocking in the dark shadows of the shrubbery that hemmed the patio, and, disconcerted, Lee caught her breath. So he'd noticed how she'd distanced herself from him earlier, even though he'd been seemingly occupied with his adoring fan.

'I wasn't aware that I was,' she bluffed, her hand going lightly to her throat. He looked dangerously handsome, a white dinner-jacket, bow-tie and black trousers enhancing that superb, innate elegance, an image that, even as he spoke, had matronly heads turning in his direction.

'It's beautiful.' Jordan's eyes had followed her nervous fingers to the dainty garnet necklace lying against the pale sheen of her skin. 'Like the woman it adorns. And as for the dress. . .' He slipped a hand into his trouser pocket, his gaze finishing what his words didn't, moving with a spine-tingling appreciation over the figure-hugging black creation she had bought in Hamilton yesterday. It had pleased her as soon as she'd tried it on, because the heavily padded shoulders seemed to balance her rather curvaceous hips, while the plunging neckline, which crossed over to tie in a belt around the midriff, did wonders for a moderate bust and also helped emphasise her tiny waist. And just for once, she thought, rather satisfyingly now, she felt a match for the tall, sophisticated Madeline. Then wondered suddenly if that was the real reason she had decided to buy it.

'So. . .you've got your story on Alec, and I believe he's asked you to spend the rest of your holiday here.' Jordan's gaze returned to her face, pale from the soul-shattering notion a moment ago that she might possibly be vying with Madeline for this man's attentions. It was ludicrous! 'I also understand that you didn't refuse.'

Because he hadn't given her the chance, waving aside her immediate negation by telling her to think it over, before wheeling himself away with a speed that had rendered the matter settled. But Vince had flown back to New York today—his work here completed— and tomorrow, when she'd added a couple of finer details to her notes, she'd be packing up, too, and getting back to the hotel.

The hidden sting in Jordan's remark, though, needled her, and she might have let it pass. But the thought of leaving in the morning made her reckless, and, with the confidence of a woman sure of her charms, she touched her tongue to red lips and purred with sublime sweetness, 'Why, Jordan? Afraid I might?'

The wind stirred the leaves of a bougainvillaea behind him, and out at sea the lights of a small yacht winked through the star-studded night. Way off, across a thousand miles of rolling ocean, lay Haiti, Antigua and Puerto Rico, names that breathed romance to her with their warm breezes and the soft hiss of the waves.

Beside her she heard Jordan's sharp intake of breath,

sensed the flexing of that powerful chest, and knew with a sweet satisfaction that her provocation had aroused the raw animal in him. The lines of his face were taut—eyelids heavy with unquestionable desire—but a discerning smile touched his lips, and his voice held a dangerous softness as his lashes came down, allowing his gaze to play across the inviting ripeness of her mouth. 'Flirting with me again, Lee?'

Danger signals went off like rockets in her brain, the sensual warning in his voice reminding her that she should have learned her lesson with him the first time. If sexuality was the weapon, then victory would be his, because in the battle between male and female he knew the rules far better than she did.

'Flattering ourselves, aren't we?' she breathed to save face, her smile brilliant, though the daggerlike quality of her gaze lost its impact when it wavered beneath the imperative strength of his. 'If you think I——'

She broke off as Madeline suddenly came up to them, and for once Lee was grateful for the other woman's presence. Another second and her ebbing confidence would have made itself quite apparent!

'Darling, so this is where you are. . .' She looked questioningly from Lee to Jordan, as though she could feel that electrifying tension, Lee thought, shuddering when the green gaze that darted back to her exhibited jealousy of an almost destructive kind. She was looking at Lee with that hard, puzzling intensity, and there was a malicious twist to her mouth, too, that made Lee uneasy.

She was glad when Alec chose that moment to join them with an entourage, and she made to excuse herself. It was Jordan they wanted to speak to, after all. But one elderly gentleman started asking her how she liked Bermuda, drawing Madeline into the conversation as well. And so politeness forced Lee to stay, so that she answered the man's questions without really taking in much of what he was saying, too aware of Jordan's too frequent glances in her direction, even though he seemed remarkably engrossed in conversation with someone else.

'. . .Mr Jackson said most of Bermuda's traditions originated in England.' It was Madeline who was recapturing her attention, the jarring tones increasing in volume, drifting too loudly across the patio. 'Well, if that's the case, then I said no one could verify that better than you. After all, that's where you come from, isn't it. . .*Coralie*?'

It was as if a thunderbolt had suddenly crashed down through the party. The talking had ceased and everyone, it seemed, was looking at Lee. She felt a pressure on her windpipe, seeing the bewildered frown on Alec's face, on the faces of the others who could sense, instinctively, that something was wrong. But it was the look on Jordan's that positively scared her.

Only a few feet away, he had gone completely white beneath his tan. His jaw—his entire body—was held rigid, the only animation in his face being his eyes, which were burning with a hard, bitter recognition.

She had to get away from him, she thought chaotically, her breath leaving her lungs on something like a tiny sob, her brain only half registering the malicious satisfaction on Madeline's face.

Murmuring some almost inaudible excuse to slip away, she turned to go inside, and finding the doorway blocked by several guests changed course, through the shrubbery, almost stumbling out into the dark, welcoming sanctuary of the garden.

How could Madeline have been so spiteful? she

thought grievously, her heart pounding as she picked out the path that fringed the trees beside the lawn, realising that the woman must have guessed her identity at some stage—if not immediately—and decided to drop her bombshell at the most embarrassing moment. *How could she have been so cruel?*

She was breathless as she came out on to the grassy slope above the small curve of the beach, seeing the moon-streaked path across the ocean through a mist of stinging tears. What she should have done was to have stayed there and faced them all, she realised hopelessly, watching the sibilant waves curling back along the sand. Instead of which she had run away like a criminal! So how could she go back and face them— Alec and Jordan—particularly Jordan—now?

She shuddered, recalling the hatred in his face, and, taking deep breaths of the salty air to steady herself, walked down on to the beach. Her high-heeled sandals sank down into the sand, and so she took them off, feeling the fine grains, cool and yielding under her bare feet. Looking up, she made a muffled sound, noticing Jordan standing on the bank immediately above her.

'So Lee Roman's Coralie Rhodes.' He spoke with a grazing softness, moving down the slope with the threatening assurance of a predator that had just spotted its prey, causing Lee's blood to freeze, fear to trickle through her. He stopped just short of the spot where the grass met the sand, his eyes trained on her face—pale and wary in the moonlight—his chest rising and falling heavily, as if she had given him a hard chase. 'I must have been an utter fool not to have realised it, but now it's all beginning to fit.' His face was grim as he thrust his hands deep into his trouser pockets, the movement exposing the leanness of his waist beneath the white jacket, the deep expanse of his chest. 'Now I see it all. . .why you've been so cagey. Your behaviour at that party. The playing up to Alec.'

'I haven't——' she started, but he didn't let her finish, his voice low and dangerous against the immutable song of the surf.

'What's wrong, *Coralie*?' He spoke her name with bitter emphasis. 'My father's funds running low? Is that why you really came here? To seduce my uncle into becoming the next unfortunate target for your greedy little schemes?'

'That's not true!' she spat at him, his words cutting deep, because he didn't know the truth. How could he? 'And if you remember, you virtually gave me no option about staying in this house. It was either that or goodbye, Lee! I would have been quite prepared to have stayed at the hotel.'

'Oh, I'm sure you would,' he accepted, almost silkily above the restless water. 'But that wouldn't have stopped you getting under his skin as you've been clever enough to do, would it?' he accused, his mouth set in hard lines. 'Or into his bed!'

Eyes blazing, Lee tasted salt on her lips, the wind ruffling the fine layers of her hair as she threw at him heatedly, 'That's disgusting!'

'Isn't it?' The hard mouth contorted unpleasantly, those perfectly moulded features half in shadow, half turned from the pale light of the moon. 'But how very like you, Coralie.'

It was pointless arguing with him while he was in this mood, she realised, afraid, especially after the way he'd seen her leaving Alec's room the other night. She could have explained, but she had made that promise to his uncle. And if he knew the financial difficulties her magazine was in he would be more convinced than ever that she was after Alec's money, she thought despairingly.

'Unfortunately for you, Alec isn't terminally sick as my father was.' Jordan's tones came unrelentingly through the cool darkness. 'He isn't going to die so *conveniently*. So what's the matter with taking on a younger man, Coralie?' The sensual threat was unmistakable even against the wash of the ocean, and her breath caught in her lungs as he began advancing. 'Or would that be more than you could handle?'

'Don't you dare!' She started to back away, the sand giving beneath her, the cold purpose in Jordan's face frightening her so much that suddenly she found herself hurling one of her shoes straight at him. He ducked, avoiding it, but still kept coming, and with a small cry she flung the other, which this time found its target and caught him squarely on the jaw. She heard his soft invective, and, panicking, broke into a run, her breath starting to burn her lungs as she sensed rather than heard him giving chase. And suddenly she let out a sharp cry of alarm, taken totally by surprise when he lunged for her ankles, whipping her legs from under her.

Breathing hard, he brought her down on the soft sand, winded but unhurt, and a small gasp left her lips as roughly he pulled her round, coming down hard on top of her.

'Jordan, no!' She wasn't sure what she feared most. His anger, or the sensations that were suddenly ripping through her from the imprisoning weight of his body, and she struggled in vain as he caught her defenceless hands to pin them on either side of her just above her head, his eyes boring deeply into the wide, frightened depths of hers.

'Oh, come on, Coralie. . .you do this for money,' he humiliated her by saying. 'And I can outstrip my father and even Alec in that department, so why not try me instead?'

As he dipped his head, in panic she jerked hers sharply to one side, staring unseeingly at the night-shrouded ocean to hiss at him through clenched teeth, 'I wouldn't want you if you were the richest man on earth!'

He laughed humourlessly, touching his lips lightly to the creamy column of her throat, the action so different from the angry assault she had been expecting that she tensed rigid, hating herself for the small sensual shiver that ran through her.

'Liar,' he whispered, aware, his breath caressing her even as it condemned. 'You want me. . .'

Trembling, afraid of the insidious pleasure he was evoking in her, she fought the bitter-sweet torment of his lips against her neck by bringing her head back swiftly, then realised that that was exactly what he had been waiting for.

With one purposeful move he captured her mouth, stifling her small protest beneath a kiss that was as earth-shattering as it was calculated. Sensations pulsed through her blood, violating all laws of logic and reason, while an instinct beyond her will had her arching her slim body even closer to the hard strength of his, her lips parting to accept the devastating invasion of her mouth. He made some sort of muffled sound, releasing her hands, and she gave a small gasp when he pressed his lower body hard against hers, awakening her startlingly to the extent of his arousal.

His lips burned against the fevered heat of her skin, down over her throat and beyond, and somehow her hands had slid beneath his jacket, exploring the hard, flexing muscles of his back. She heard him groan, and then his mouth clamped over hers again, and she was drowning beneath his kiss. Anger had fuelled his passion, but now passion sought only to feed itself, its hunger fierce and mutual and which had her breathing as raggedly as he was, moving sensuously against him, all rational thought swamped by the bruising insistence of his mouth, by his hard hands, her mind as abandoned as the wind and the surging sea.

One hand pushed aside the soft fabric of her dress, and she gave a sharp, shocked gasp as his fingers closed around the soft mound of her breast, fondling and tormenting, her untutored body jerking in a spasm as his mouth followed the pathway of his hand, teasing the sensitive, hardening peak with its moist warmth until coils of need became an intensifying ache deep in her loins.

Oh, *please*. . .

Just when she thought she would die of wanting, he was lifting his head, his face muscles taut as he looked down at her lying beneath him, seeming almost to want to engorge his senses with everything about her; her slumbrous eyes, her perfume, the way her breasts lifted sharply from her quick, erratic breathing, the creamy texture of the flesh he had exposed, tinged with the flush of desire.

'Hell! How do those older men cope with that passionate nature, Coralie?' he breathed, his voice rough, husky from his own basic need of her. 'Or is that another thing you've sacrificed along with your self-respect?'

His scathing remark dragged her out of her reckless ardour. Pride stinging, she pushed at him, then realised he was rolling away of his own accord because someone was calling his name.

'Mr Colyer! Mr Colyer! Telephone call for you.' Somehow Lee managed to follow his example and get to her feet, hurriedly grappling with her dress as Alec's manservant came into view. 'I wouldn't have bothered you, bit it's an overseas call. . .'

'That's all right, Matthew.' Jordan sounded calm, remarkably composed, while Lee toyed with her necklace agitatedly, her face half turned from the grey-haired man, ashamed that he might have witnessed what was going on. 'We'd better go back,' Jordan suggested as the other man retreated, his voice cool and amazingly steady after the raw passion that had gripped him a few moments before. 'We'll talk inside.'

As he took her arm, Lee pulled roughly away from him, her face flushed against a wild cloud of dark hair.

'I've got nothing to say to you!' she spat, still breathing irregularly, the way she had responded to his lovemaking when his contempt for her was so obvious making her wish only for tomorrow when she could leave, so that she wouldn't have to face him again.

'No, I don't suppose you have,' he agreed witheringly. 'Nevertheless, I want to talk to you. I also think you might have the decency to do a little explaining to Alec.'

He was right, of course, but a coil of apprehension made her feel sick inside. She didn't think she could face the older man—not yet. Not after the way she had unintentionally deceived him when he'd been so kind to her. But she said, truculently, 'Then you'll just have to go on wanting, won't you? And anything I have to say to Alec is entirely between him and me. Go and answer your caller, Jordan,' she recommended coolly, in an endeavour to appear calmer than she was feeling after that mortifying need for him that had had her in its treacherous talons just now. 'I'm sure it must be costing them a fortune.'

In the pale light of the moon, his face was etched

with harsh lines, and for a moment she feared that he was going to insist she accompany him back by carrying her up the beach. It was a relief, therefore, when, with lips compressed in angry compliance, he turned and strode away from her, leaving her feeling wretched and thoroughly ashamed.

Defeatedly, she hunted around for her shoes. She found them easily after a few moments, because they showed up darkly against the moon-bleached sand, but she still didn't feel like going back to the house. Virtually everyone on the patio had known something was wrong when Madeline had delivered her condemning little speech—even if they hadn't known what it was—and, after the way she had run away like that, curiosities would be aroused. So, with a shoe in each hand, she started walking unhappily along the beach, her heart heavy with despair.

Why, oh, why was she so attracted to him? she interrogated herself hopelessly, the salt sea-air dampening her hair, making it soft and fluffy against her shoulders. He hated her, and she wasn't particularly enamoured with him either, so what sort of game was fate playing with her to make her want him with an intensity that had been almost beyond her control? When there was no way that she could make him believe that she wasn't the person he liked to think she was? Convincing him that there was nothing between her and Alec would be easy enough, she realised, kicking at the sand. He'd only have to ask his uncle to find out the truth. But the question of his father, she reflected, staring ahead at the dark, shadowy rocks at the end of the little beach, was quite a different story. . .

And then she felt it. The danger that was suddenly snaking towards her. She turned, letting out a scream that was instantly stifled as the danger became a physical presence. She struggled against the dark figure that was suddenly threatening her very existence, and felt the dainty garnet necklace being torn from her neck. She smelt alcohol, reeking unpleasantly close to her face, then a sharp, piercing blow sliced across her temple. She toppled backwards, thinking, 'This is it— it's all over,' hearing only the sea gushing in her ears as she fell on to the damp sand, and then nothing.

CHAPTER SIX

HANDS that were strong and unyielding were upon her
again, pulling her out of the merciful blackness into
nightmarish reality. She uttered a small sound and tried
to fight with what little strength she had, realising, even
in her semi-conscious state, that it was futile. The man
was too strong.

'It's all right, Coralie! It's all right.' Jordan's voice
was urgent, then soothing when she recognised it
enough to stop fighting him, and gently she was eased
up out of the sand. 'It's all right, Coralie. It's all right.'

The comforting familiarity of someone she knew,
even if it was him, was too much for her, and she was
sobbing quietly into the warm curve of his neck,
overwhelmed by relief at recognising his scent, feeling
the sure protection of his arms around her.

'Jordan. . .'

'It's all right. You're safe,' he was reassuring her
again. 'Alec was worried sick about you. You've been
gone for nearly two hours.' And he? Had he been
worried about her? She was too weak to stop the
thought forming in her mind, or even to ask herself
why she should care. 'For heaven's sake! Who did
this?' he demanded, as he began carrying her along the
beach. As if she could tell him!

'A shape. . .that's all I remember,' she uttered, her
head throbbing. It was such an effort to speak. 'He
took my necklace. . .'

'Is that all you're worried about?' His dry, clipped

comment reminded her of how materialistic he considered her, and, involuntarily, she shivered. 'If you hadn't noticed, he gave you a very nice crack on the head!'

She didn't have the energy to tell him that she *had* noticed! Her head felt as if it had been split in two. It was as much as she could do to sob an almost inaudible, 'Why?'

'You're in a rich man's playground, Coralie. Pink sand and moonlight don't make it any safer than New York.'

She supposed he was right, and from some other time remembered him almost insisting she accompany him back to the house. Had he, in spite of everything then, been concerned for her welfare?

'What's wrong? What happened? Is she all right?' Alec's worried tones drifted up to her as Jordan carried her through the patio doors, the lack of any other voices assuring her that all the guests had gone. There was no sign of Madeline.

'Yes, just a bump on the head. But you'd better call Henderson to take a look at her.'

'No, I'm all right. . .' Lee began to protest, but gave a small groan as she tried to lift her head from Jordan's shoulder.

'Who are you trying to convince? Yourself?' His grim scepticism was all she needed as he bore her effortlessly upstairs, shouldering his way into her bedroom. 'This time, Coralie, you're going to do as you're told.'

She was too weak to argue against his censuring strength, yet when he placed her gently on the bed and stood up, strangely she felt the loss of his arms. His neck-tie had been discarded and his shirt was half buttoned beneath his jacket, she noticed now, as if he'd been intending to go to bed himself before he'd decided to come looking for her.

'I think we'd better get you out of this.' He was looking at the sorry state of her dress, but as he moved to put his words into action Lee shrank away from him, her eyes dark and horrified against the pallor of her face.

'No!'

'Modesty, Coralie?' Irony curled his mouth. 'I would have thought you'd traded that a long time ago. Shall I call one of the maids to help you?'

She ignored the barbed comment, in no shape to retaliate, her aversion to being undressed by him springing solely from the shaming memory of the intimacy she had allowed him earlier on the beach. 'No, I can manage.'

As though to allow her a few moments' privacy, he went through into the bathroom, and with a great effort that made her wish she'd agreed to his suggestion and enlisted someone's help, Lee managed to peel off the damp garment. In the room beyond she could hear the click of a cupboard door, then water running, and when Jordan returned she had somehow managed to slip under the duvet.

'Let's look at that wound.' He set a shallow dish down on the bedside cabinet, steam rising from it with the strong odour of antiseptic. Then, throwing his jacket over a chair, he came and sat down beside her on the edge of the bed, the mattress depressing under his weight. He tilted her chin to examine the dark red gash on her right temple, at the same time moistening a cotton wool pad in the warm water. 'This might hurt a little.'

He was right. As the antiseptic touched her wound, it stung viciously, and she sucked in her breath.

'I'm sorry.' He paused, hand suspended, waiting for the stinging to subside, his gaze meeting hers with such directness that she was forced to lower her own. He was having to lean across her to bathe the gash, and as he reapplied the cotton wool with surprising care her numbed senses were sharply awakened to the hard warmth of him against her, that evocative male scent of him, and the quiet regularity of his breathing.

Needing to say something because he wasn't, after a few moments, she asked feebly, 'Why didn't you just leave me there? I'd have thought you'd have considered it my just desserts.'

He brought his arm down on the bed. 'Don't think I didn't consider it.' With marked precision he tossed the cotton-wool pad into a wicker basket several yards away, and turned back to her, a muscle tugging in his jaw. 'Unlike you, Coralie, I happen to have too much of a conscience to leave someone to suffer alone, regardless of how little I may respect them.'

She already knew what he thought of her, but being told was like a rub-down with a block of ice. Goose-pimples broke out all over her body, making her shiver, so that he was suddenly palming her forehead, his fingers cool on her feverish skin. 'Are you feeling all right?'

She nodded, even though she wasn't, thinking she must look a fright, too, with her hair hanging limply around her face and her mascara probably streaked from where she had been crying. But, oddly that last action of his brought tears to her eyes again, and as he got up to clear away the dish, and pick up her dress, tremulously she uttered, 'I know you'll never accept a thing I say, but, believe it or not, I liked *and* respected your father.'

His expression criticised as he looked down at her,

the dish in one hand, her dress over the same arm. And he said, quietly, 'A fine way you had of showing it, Coralie, going off and enjoying yourself while he died in that hospital—alone—without a soul.'

Even after eight years, surprisingly, the pain was still there, in his face—his voice. Lee stared up at him with hurt, questioning eyes, her fingers twisting absently in the duvet. Hadn't *he* been there? She'd always imagined that he had.

'I didn't know,' she started to say, but her feeble attempt was cut short by the arrival of the doctor, a stocky, bald-headed man who instantly diagnosed concussion and recommended she be hospitalised for observation immediately.

'I don't need that,' she dissented, the dizziness as she tried to sit up making her realise that she probably did, and so she didn't object when Jordan sent for a maid to help her dress.

'No,' he said firmly, when he returned and saw that she was intending to try and walk downstairs herself. As if she were a helpless child, he wrapped a rug around her and carried her down to the car.

She didn't remember anything about that journey, exhausted sleep claiming her long before they reached the hospital. But on arrival she underwent the most stringent tests, with even more the following morning, and afterwards the police arrived with endless questions, although she didn't feel she was much help to them as she couldn't really give them much of a description of the man who had mugged her. Then, much later, just as a nurse finished taking her temperature, she had another visitor.

'Feeling better?' Alec enquired, smiling at the nurse who held the door open for him so he could manoeuvre his chair into the little private ward.

Lee nodded, racked with guilt. He must still be feeling baffled—utterly deceived—she thought, with a pang of miserable conscience, and last night she hadn't been in a fit state to try and explain to him.

'Matthew brought me,' he informed her then, making her blush to realise that, unwittingly, she'd glanced over his head, expecting to see Jordan.

'Oh,' she said quietly, and wasn't sure whether she was relieved or disappointed.

'I rang first thing and the doctor told me that everything seems to be in order.' He sounded immensely relieved himself, and Lee followed his gaze to the young nurse who was filling in her chart, realising how much trouble she had caused everyone. 'They want to keep you in until tomorrow morning, though, so you'll have to be patient a little while longer.'

Obviously he could sense her restlessness to be up and about again, and she smiled wanly at his understanding.

'I'm sorry,' she said, after a moment, running her finger absently over the edge of the crisp white sheet.

'For getting a bump on the head?' Silver eyebrows lifted. 'That was hardly your fault.'

'No, not for that.' Nerves clutched at her stomach, and she sent a hesitant glance towards the other girl, who smiled pleasantly, and then went out. 'I didn't mean to deceive anyone,' she elucidated then, deciding to offer her explanations before Alec could start demanding them. She looked at him with apologetic eyes, dark underneath from the previous night's ordeal, her face pale in contrast. 'When I came here I didn't have a clue that you were Jordan's uncle. I'd never have asked you to see me if I had. And whatever Jordan's told you. . .I didn't live with his father,' she stressed. 'Not in the way you must think, anyway.' She caught her breath as she moved her head too quickly. It throbbed a little less this morning, but was still rather sensitive. 'He was more like an uncle to me than anything else, and he just gave me a home when Dad died, that's all. When he left me all that money. . .' Her hands splayed themselves hopelessly against the bedspread. 'Well. . .I didn't expect anything like that! But I don't expect you to believe me. Why should you? You probably think exactly the same as Jordan, and I'm sorry if you do, but that's all I can say.'

The man's brow furrowed as he sat with his elbows on the steel arms of his chair, hands clasped against his chest.

'I don't want explanations about the past, Lee,' he said soberly. 'It's over and done with. And, anyway, it's Jordan you're going to have to convince, not me.' And after a moment, 'You do realise, with my nephew, that it wasn't ever the money he objected to you having?' His eyes were clear and steady, silently judging her. 'Only the way in which he thought you had come by it.'

Of course she realised that. Even then, eight years ago, young as she was, she'd known it wasn't just the money.

'But he was wrong about me,' she said emphatically, wondering if she could even convince Alec. It seemed totally futile, she decided, uttering sadly after a few moments, 'If you don't want me to go ahead with the feature, I fully understand.'

'Have I said that?' His swift rejoinder brought her gaze up from the large pink flowers on the bedspread.

'You mean. . .you believe me?' she exhaled, eyes incredulous.

Outside, a car engine purred into life, and closer to hand footsteps hurried down the corridor.

'I'd like to believe you wouldn't lie to me, Lee.' Blue
eyes regarded her obliquely, his mouth moving in a
wry curve. 'Or is it Coralie now?'

'Whatever you like,' she uttered resignedly, unable
to comprehend why Alec wasn't judging her quite so
harshly as his nephew had. 'Coralie Rhodes just didn't
seem as businesslike as Lee Roman—that's the only
reason I changed it.'

He acknowledged this with a brief nod. Then he
surprised her by saying, 'And you'll accept my hospitality for the rest of your holiday?'

Lee stared at him, disbelievingly. 'But I can't!' she
breathed, catching the fragrance of a lemony-scented
shrub growing just outside the window. 'It wouldn't be
right and——'

'I think you owe it to me, Lee.' There was a soft
reproof in his words which brought colour into her pale
cheeks. She supposed she did, in a way. She didn't feel
particularly proud of the way she had kept her real
identity from him. 'Besides, I'd like to get to know the
girl my brother-in-law cared enough about to share his
home with.'

Lee hesitated, swallowing. She knew she should be
grateful that, at the very least, he wasn't censuring a
near-week's work. But staying under the same roof
with Jordan now that he knew who she was! And
particularly after that shameful response to him last
night! She didn't think she could.

'Jordan doesn't want me there,' she decided to
remind him, just in case he'd overlooked that little
point.

The man gave one of his contemptuous snorts that
he usually reserved for Arlene. 'It's my house,' was his
swift response. Then he startled her by asking pointedly, 'Are you afraid of him?'

He was leaning forward in his chair, and she swore those piercing blue eyes were quite aware of the colour that crept along her cheekbones from the way her blood pulsed through her, because she was afraid of Jordan—or rather, the soul-shattering attraction he held for her, if not the man himself. But, somewhat defensively, she answered, 'No,' and saw a muscle twitch at the side of Alec's mouth as if he didn't quite believe her.

'Then I'll see you tomorrow,' he said, in that firm, dismissive way of his, grasping the opportunity of another nurse's arrival to assist him through the door. And, with a parting glance over his shoulder, 'I'll send Matthew to pick you up.'

Waiting in the busy reception area the following morning, Lee glanced up as the outside doors swung open and Jordan strode in, looking magnificent in a light, short-sleeved shirt and navy cords.

'Is anything the matter?' he quizzed, when he saw the surprised look on her face.

'No,' she answered, getting up from her chair, that familiar, disquieting tension ebbing through her blood. 'I was expecting Matthew, that's all.'

He pushed open the swing door for her with a pleasant waft of cologne, saying rather dispassionately, 'I'm sorry to disappoint you.'

She didn't answer him as she stepped out into the sunny car park. She didn't see any point.

Apart from asking her how she was as she got into the car, he didn't say anything else to her, and she guessed he'd only said that much because those superlative manners of his demanded it. Yet they'd told her in the hospital that he'd carried her in the other night, and she considered that he must have handled her with unbelievable care because she hadn't stirred until the doctor had come along—hadn't seen him go. But he would probably have done it for anyone, no matter what he thought about them, she was quick to assure herself in case she started getting any fancy ideas about his motives, and with a mental shrug she looked out of the window as the powerful car growled through Bermuda's only city.

In Hamilton harbour the water was a vivid blue against the colourful sails of yachts and other small craft, and the breathtaking magnitude of a cruise ship that had just come in. Closer to hand, horse-drawn carriages stood in the shade along the tree-lined street, a throw-back to the days when they were the islanders' only form of transport, yet which now provided an exciting diversion for tourists. Shops, cafés and other more official-looking buildings breathed life like any other city, while a policeman in dark Bermuda shorts and a traditionally English helmet directed traffic through the busy street.

'Have the police been back to you since yesterday?' Obviously Jordan had been aware of what was absorbing her interest.

She turned to look at him, her hair a dark contrast against the pale lemon leisure-suit she was wearing. 'No.' A thin line creased her forehead, smooth and flawless save for the dark bruising around her temple. 'Have you heard anything?'

He braked hard, reflexes lightning swift as the car in front suddenly pulled up without any warning, and he cursed softly under his breath. 'They think they've got a lead,' he said phlegmatically, changing gear, adding on a long, hard breath, 'Thankfully.' The poignancy in his voice had her questioning the inscrutable lines of his profile as he negotiated the final junction out of

Hamilton. 'It had crossed my mind that I might possibly have been considered chief suspect.' His gaze fell to the silent, appalled query in hers, and he said drily, 'I *was* the last person to see you alone before Matthew came down to fetch me that night. Or had you forgotten?'

A flame of colour spread up Lee's throat into her cheeks, and, embarrassed, she stared down at the soft towelling of her leisure-suit. How could she have forgotten that? His pulsing anger as he'd brought her down in the sand; the firm insistence of his mouth over hers; the hard, demanding strength of his body. . .

She felt the glance he directed her way, but couldn't bring herself to look up, shamefully aware of how she had invited his kisses, the arousing intimacy of his hands. And beside her she heard him say, 'I'm surprised you didn't take the opportunity to suggest as much to the police. I was rather expecting you might.'

She stared at him incredulously, her pale features criss-crossed by the dappled sunlight that shone down through the trees at the side of the road. Was his opinion of her that low?

'Don't worry,' she mollified bitterly, with a glance over the casual shirt which hugged those powerful muscles. 'I told them he was shorter than you—and thinner.' And that was all she could recollect about the man, besides that reek of alcohol, although those moments when she had been under attack had seemed like an eternity. A cold, queasy fear infiltrated her blood as she remembered how she had struggled, the unyielding strength of the man before he had hit her over the head, her terror. . .

'Do you want some fresh air?' In a sick daze, she realised that Jordan was already stopping the car, and it was as much as she could do to nod, her cheeks drained of all colour. She felt damp, cold with sweat, and slightly faint. 'Come on.'

His voice was gentle as he helped her out, and he supported her while she took lungfuls of the sweet warm air, which was freshened by the breeze in the leafy lane. The arms she clung to were strong and warm and reassuring, and gradually the faintness began to subside.

'I'm all right.' Alarmed to find her hands resting against the soft cotton of his shirt, she tried to pull back from him, but he was employing the minimum of strength to draw her slight frame against the hard solidity of his. His mouth was moist and warm on hers—unbelievably gentle—respecting her present frailty. But when his eyes came into focus again they bore none of the tenderness of his kiss, and there was a tightness about his face, self-condemnation in every taut line, that told her he wanted her—and hated himself because of it.

Lee tugged away from him and got into the car, hurting as if he'd slapped her.

'What's wrong, Coralie?' His smile was cruelly derisive as he looked down at her through the open door. 'Wasn't getting involved with me in your plans?'

He had closed the door before she could say anything, and anyway it would have been pointless, after the other night, to deny how strongly she was attracted to him. But her own weakness for him, coupled with that scathing remark, burned into her pride, so that as soon as he was beside her again she retaliated, 'Do you really think I came here to try and seduce Alec for. . .money? That's just about the level I'd expect your brain to function at! Well, fortunately, he's got a greater capacity for understanding than you!'

'Yes,' he averred heavily, turning towards her.

'Whatever little sob story you spun him in that hospital yesterday, he's chosen to believe, but if you've plans on winding up in anyone's bed while you're here, Coralie, you'd better know now, it's going to be mine.'

'You conceited. . .' Angry colour throbbed into her cheeks and temples from the sheer audacity of the man, but more from the unsettling imagery of his last statement.

'No, not conceited, little Eve,' he corrected with quietly controlled anger. 'Just making sure you don't use Alec the way you used my father. And if it means teaching you a few lessons in humility, it'll be worth every minute of my time!' She started to say something, but he cut in, not giving her the chance. 'Tell me one thing, Coralie. . .does it ever prick your conscience that you were dancing in another man's arms the night your lover died?'

'He wasn't my lover!' she threw at him vehemently. 'Although you're obviously eaten up by some problem of your own to ever want to believe that!' She saw his eyes darken, a muscle pull in his jaw as though she had touched a raw nerve, but she carried on regardless, pushed to the limit. 'Well, frankly, I don't give a damn what you believe! I don't know why he left me that money. I wish the hell he hadn't! But, just for the record, he made me take that holiday. I don't know why. I can only guess it was because he didn't want me around when——' She broke off, drawing a deep breath, her eyes holding his in a staunch refusal to be intimidated. 'Anyway, I didn't realise he was ill, or he could never have made me go. I *didn't know*.'

A dark eyebrow lifted, scepticism in every line of that strong, masculine face. 'Madeline knew.' His voice was as accusing as the penetrating darkness of his eyes, and Lee let out an exasperated breath, feeling as if she

were banging her head against a stone wall. Already it
was beginning to throb.

'She was his confidante!' she stressed passionately.
'Someone he always turned to—who'd been loyal to
him for years.' Which was probably why the woman
had been so vindictive towards her, Lee thought, when
that loyalty had been rewarded in a way which, though
generous, could never have compared with the huge
sum Richard had left *her*. 'Besides, I wasn't much more
than a child,' her small chin lifted in wounded accusation to his, 'as you so cruelly took great pleasure in
pointing out!'

Surprisingly, he remembered that unkind criticism,
as one glance over her now pleasingly feminine figure
testified. And just that brief, visual caress had her
heartbeat accelerating—her blood racing through her.
But she was feeling weary, too, and a little bit sick,
and he must have been sensitive to that, if nothing
else, she realised, because, with one look at her wan
features, he was saying swiftly, 'I'd better get you
home.'

She still hadn't managed to convince him, she
thought hopelessly, as he put the car into motion, and
she decided that it was a waste of time trying. Alec, for
some reason, had believed her, and he might have
thought she could make Jordan believe her, too, but
his mind was too closed against her even to hope to.
And she didn't get another opportunity, because as
soon as they reached the house he received a telephone
call necessitating his immediate departure for New
York, so that, an hour later, he left, taking Madeline
with him.

CHAPTER SEVEN

LEE relaxed against the sun-lounger under the shade of the poinciana, alone, as Matthew had taken his employer out on the boat. The last three days, she thought fondly, had been a period of recuperation under the paternal eye of her host, when she had walked and swum and sketched—as she was doing now—or simply soaked up the sun.

'You've got a tan already,' Arlene had said to her that morning, during a break from putting Alec through his paces. Lee smiled as she remembered the familiar, harmless banter that had followed between therapist and patient, a banter she was becoming accustomed to, and which was a constant source of amusement to her. As for Jordan, the house lacked his presence, she thought, somewhat reluctantly, getting back to her sketch, finding herself anticipating his return as much as she dreaded it. And in that instant she started, glancing up to see him looking over her shoulder.

'It's good.' She blushed, instantly self-conscious of her meagre attempt to capture the poolside, but he was surveying her work with the keen interest of a serious critic and so she held it up for him to study more closely, her pulse galloping. She hadn't seen him since the day he had brought her back from the hospital, and now, in spite of herself, all she wanted was to absorb every last detail of him: the way his hair fell tantalisingly across his forehead, how those long, black lashes cast shadows against the wells of his eyes, the hard structure of his cheek and jawline, and the firm, commanding mouth which was compressing now in obvious appreciation of her work. 'It's very good,' he expanded frankly, such rare praise from him, coupled with his nearness, sending an odd warmth tingling through her. 'Why aren't you on the boat with Alec?' He came around the side of the lounger, his expression curious. 'When I telephoned this morning he said he was going to do a spot of reef fishing. Why didn't you go with him?'

Unconsciously, Lee traced the outline of her bottom lip with the end of her pencil, then, seeing the way Jordan's eyes followed the gesture, quickly desisted, realising how provocative it could seem.

'I don't like bloodsports,' she blurted out somewhat belligerently, although, that morning, not wanting to offend Alec after all his kindness, she had told him a little white lie and said that she got a bit queasy on the water. She half expected Jordan to oppose her views. But he didn't.

Instead, his mouth moved in a contemplative smile, his gaze flickering briefly over her pale lemon sun-top and white shorts, before he said with a mocking softness, 'Scruples, Coralie?' as though mildly surprised to discover that she did have some. She tensed, piqued by his continuous need to taunt her. But before she could retaliate he was saying, 'Still, it's a far more creditable reason than not wanting to ruin your hairdo.'

Is that what Madeline would have said? Unwittingly, she darted a glance towards the house.

'No, Coralie,' he said quietly, 'Madeline didn't come back with me.'

She looked at him quickly from behind her sunglasses, colour rushing to her cheeks, disconcerted that

he should so easily have guessed what she was thinking—that she should even care! And then, to her
surprise, he reached down to tilt her chin to one side,
the light touch of his fingers sending shock-waves
through her. 'It's healing nicely.'

'Yes.' She sounded ridiculously breathless.

For a moment his eyes locked with hers, those dark
depths smouldering with something so intimate and
primeval that she felt the hard throb of her pulse. But
then he straightened, his gaze moving casually over her
again, before he said matter-of-factly, 'Alec also told
me he's had the police on the phone. That they wanted
to know if you're up to attending an identification
parade yet, to try and pick up the man they think might
have attacked you. *And* to recovering your necklace—
if you feel up to it.'

A cold, sick feeling shuddered through her. Numbly,
she stared down at her sketch-pad, the colour leaving
her cheeks. They had telephoned this morning, and
last night, but she didn't think she would ever be up to
it—facing her attacker. Pointing him out in cold blood.
Not that she'd ever recognise the man, anyway.

A bird swooped low, gliding over the pool like an
iridescent flame, and absently Lee watched it, her face
taut with anxiety.

'I can't,' she whispered, without looking at him,
ashamed of her faint-heartedness in front of him. She
doubted if a man like that ever experienced fear.

'Wouldn't it be best to get it over with?' The
Canadian tones were surprisingly soft—devoid all at
once of any condemnation—as though he understood.
'You could help prevent the same thing happening
again, you know—to someone else.'

He was right, of course. He moved slightly, his
shadow falling across her, bringing her attention to the

superb physical power of him in the casual shirt and dark trousers.

'Do you want me to come with you?'

His suggestion brought her surprised gaze to his, her chest lifting in rebellion against it. But she knew she couldn't do it alone, and she was silently grateful to him when he didn't wait for her to openly admit to needing him, but said simply, 'Go and get dressed. I'll see you in the car.'

It was a waste of time, as she had known it would be, although more of an ordeal than she had ever imagined, and when she came out of the identification-room, pale from confronting what had seemed a parade of hostile faces, to her utter mortification she was close to breaking down. Half aware, she heard one of the officers offering to help her—to get her a cup of tea—while somehow she found herself in Jordan's arms, not really knowing how she got there, her face against the comforting strength of his shoulder.

'It's all right. . .I'll take care of it.' His tone, as he addressed the policemen, was deep and dismissive, and blindly Lee let him lead her outside.

The air was refreshing and she gulped at it as if it were a life-saver, and after a few moments heard Jordan say quietly, 'Let's go for a drive, shall we?'

His depth of understanding was something new she learnt about him that afternoon, because he seemed to know exactly how to deal with her. First in her need to say nothing, and then in the way he gradually drew her out of herself, cleverly inducing her to talk about that night on the beach, until it all came pouring out of her—the fear and the terror—so that she was amazed by how much she told him—and how easily he listened. Afterwards, though, she felt oddly cleansed, and a

little later—probably when he felt the time was right—
he took a small brown envelope out of his shirt pocket.

'Here.' His eyes left the road only briefly as he
handed it to her. Her necklace, she discovered, opening it. She hardly remembered signing for it, and
guessed the officer had given it to Jordan as she had
been in such a sorry state, and carefully she tipped out
the priceless little piece of jewellery—priceless to her,
anyway.

It felt cold, sparkling with a gentle brilliance in the
sun, and she held it up, draped gently over her palm.
Every small, delicate stone was there, but the slim,
silver catch was broken, and without warning tears
welled into her eyes, so that she stared out at a blur of
red hibiscus blooms which were growing in the hedge-
row, hoping Jordan wouldn't notice. But, of course, he
did.

'Did he mean that much to you?'

Lee caught her breath, tensing beneath her pale blue
cotton dress. Naturally, he'd assumed it was from some
man!

'Yes,' she answered simply, still looking ahead. 'He
was my father.'

She felt his eyes on her again—dark and contemplative—but he didn't say anything, and she knew a small
element of satisfaction in guessing that he was probably
lost for words in realising he'd been wrong.

He was overtaking two cyclists on the narrow road,
and, pulling in again, send a sidelong glance towards
the necklace. 'Does it have a history?' Clearly, he had
an eye for an antique.

'It was my grandmother's.' Carefully, Lee put the
necklace back into the envelope, tucking it safely away
in a pocket of her handbag.

'Oh?' The dark profile tilted in her direction again.
'And was she anything like you?'

She didn't know whether he meant that in a detrimental or a complimentary way but, snapping her handbag closed, she answered, 'I don't remember much about her. She died when I was quite small. We were born on the same day, though—Midsummer's Day—and so my parents named me after her. The necklace was a wedding present from her late husband—my grandfather—and she asked my father to give it to me when I was old enough to appreciate it, which he did—on my sixteenth birthday.' She concluded on an almost sad note, 'It was the only thing of any real value he ever owned.'

She felt Jordan's assessing glance, and wondered if he was thinking that it was obviously that humble background of hers that had made his own father such an attractive prospect for her. But he said only, 'I'm glad you've got it back,' yet with such genuine sincerity that she didn't know how to respond, suddenly not sure of him any more.

He took her for a long drive along the South Shore Road, overlooking what had to be the most beautiful beaches in the world—such as Marley and Coral Beach, and the beckoning curve of Horseshoe Bay, where yuccas and other tropical shrubs yielded to the sturdy supremacy of the palm. Out in the turquoise water stretched miles and miles of reef, and seeing her interest Jordan said laconically, 'It's known as "The Boilers",' and she could see why. The surf breaking along it was a continual mass of bubbling white foam.

A colony of modern pink holiday cottages met them as they travelled on, their gardens sloping away to lush hillside and coral sand, and the glittering gold of the ocean.

'Mark Twain called it heaven.'

She glanced up to meet Jordan's mocking awareness of the pleasure that lit her face.

'The Spanish, on the other hand, weren't so complimentary. They preferred to think of the place as "the Isles of the Devil".'

'Oh?' Lee looked at him interestedly as he changed gear to take a road inland.

'They lost too many ships on the reefs, and therefore deduced that the islands had to be haunted—plagued by evil spirits,' he enlightened her, his chuckle softening the proud austerity of his profile, 'so they wouldn't settle here. That's why your countrymen took residence instead, but credit for discovery, Coralie, really lies with the Spanish, not the British.'

She hadn't realised that. Impressed, she turned away, wondering why he seemed more tolerant towards her today. Perhaps he just felt sorry for her in view of what she had been through, she thought. Or perhaps, by some miracle, her outburst the other day had started him thinking that he might possibly have been wrong about her all these years. Oh, heaven, she hoped so! And realised then that she wanted his respect more than she had ever wanted anything.

'I think it's time we——' Whatever he had been about to say was cut short as he brought the car out of a bend and had to brake unexpectedly behind a sudden build-up of crawling traffic. Ahead, Lee could see some sort of activity going on—people lining the roadside— and now, through the open window, she caught the unmistakable sound of drums.

'Gombeys,' Jordan announced laconically, in answer to her questioning glance, but rather impatiently, too, as though he had something else on his mind and didn't want to be bothered with having to pull in as he was being forced to do. 'Come along,' he said, with almost weary acceptance, clicking his seat-belt free, then leaning across to release hers, the casual brush of his arm against her breast making her breath catch in her lungs. 'It's something not to be missed.'

He was right about that. Almost pulled after him past a row of parked cars, Lee could feel the excitement in the air as they joined the throng gathering further along the road, while all the time the beat of the drums drew nearer.

From her place in the crowd, in an atmosphere of eager anticipation, Lee watched as the carnival-like procession suddenly came into view, native Bermudians in an extravaganza of costume and dance, their superb dark bodies twisting in a frenzy of expression. Tassels and fringes, sequins and beads created a blaze of colour, while grotesque masks yielded to spectacular head-dresses of feathers and tiny mirrors that threw back the dazzling sunlight with their wild dancing.

People were throwing coins that tinkled across the sun-baked tarmac, and Jordan slipped a hand into his pocket, following their example.

'It's an island tradition that always takes place at Christmastime and now, during heritage month,' he told Lee at her shoulder. 'The more money that's thrown, the faster they're supposed to move.'

It was a paganlike ritual that was primitive and enthralling—part of Bermuda's past—and Lee laughed, glad that she hadn't missed it—glad, too, that for a while, at least, Jordan wasn't flaying her with that cold contempt.

Beside them, a young woman holding a toddler was trying to find a clear view for a slightly older child who was whimpering because he couldn't see, and Lee was surprised when, after exchanging a word with the young mother, Jordan stooped and swung the little boy up on to his shoulder. Blushing, the woman thanked him, and Lee noticed how her gaze stole in his direction from time to time, obviously appreciating the man's dark good looks, while her son, too, seemed more interested in this new hunk of masculinity than in the Gombeys, who were passing now with a crescendo of drumming and frenetic movement, because, after a bout of initial shyness, the boy was chattering unreservedly to him.

Lee noted how Jordan responded, not with the usual patronising tone a lot of adults used with little ones, but with a warm indulgence that was open and friendly, and which sent a swell of inexplicable emotion through her that made her ache for some little token of affection from him herself.

'I didn't know you liked children,' she couldn't help remarking afterwards, when they were walking back through the dispersing crowd.

'There's probably quite a lot you don't know about me, Coralie,' he stated with an edge to his voice, the wind lifting his black hair as he stooped to unlock the car.

Yes, like why you aren't married, she thought, over the slamming of other vehicles' doors and the now fading Gombey drums. Why you haven't got kids of your own. Because she couldn't help having decided that he'd probably make a marvellous father, when he did eventually settle down with a wife, and couldn't stop herself wondering whether Madeline Eastman would be the one to fill that role.

Her spirits were considerably lowered when they got back on the road again, so that she scarcely noticed the sudden lack of houses, or the narrow lane Jordan pulled into, until he stopped the car outside a small stone cottage.

'I bought it as a holiday retreat years ago,' he explained to Lee's silent query, 'although since Alec moved here, and particularly since his accident, whenever I come here I tend to stay with him. I like to pop down here sometimes, though, and give the place an airing—see if there's any sort of post. Come on. I'll make you some coffee.'

There was no post, just some unsolicited advertising leaflets which he screwed up without even reading them, before showing her into the lounge. 'Do you mind dried milk?'

She shook her head, looking around as he went through into the kitchen.

There were cottage colonies all over the island like the ones they had passed earlier. But this house was a one-off, older and with much more character reflected in its cedar beams and huge stone fireplace, the very privacy of the place, with its comfortable classic furniture and homely atmosphere, giving rise to the intrusive thought of whether he ever brought Madeline here.

The conclusion was more depressing than Lee wanted to admit, and she shook it aside as a collection of small, framed oil-paintings caught her attention on the far wall.

It wasn't until she heard Jordan say, 'What do you think?' that she swung round, realising they had been absorbing her interest for all the time it had taken him to make the coffee.

'They're lovely. So. . .vital!' she breathed, taking one of the steaming mugs he handed her. It wasn't an artist she was familiar with, she thought, struggling to make out the signature on one of them, but definitely one of considerable talent, the brushwork fine and detailed, every stroke the handiwork of an artist destined to go far.

'They were done by my mother.' His casual remark had her pivoting round, lips parting in amazement. His *mother*! No wonder he'd shown such a keen interest in her own little sketch. 'She had quite a promising career before she was married.'

And had died tragically in a fire, Lee remembered Richard telling her once—not long after Jordan was born.

'She was very talented,' said Lee quietly, sipping her coffee carefully because the dried milk hadn't done anything to cool it.

He didn't say anything, regarding her slim figure over the rim of his mug with such blatant thoroughness that she blushed, and took a swift, extra-large gulp of her coffee.

'Sit down,' he advised quietly, while she was doing her utmost to conceal the discomfort of a burnt tongue. She complied, choosing the chintzy settee, which was a mistake, she decided, when he deposited himself on the arm, only a foot or so away from her. 'Tell me about *your* mother.'

She looked at him obliquely. 'Why?' she quizzed, reluctant to discuss a subject that was both personal and painful to her. 'Are you hoping I'll say she disowned me because she disapproved of me living with an older man?' She saw a muscle pull in the strong jaw, the inexorable features forcing her to add, 'Well, for your information, Jordan, it was before that, back in England.'

A little furrow creased her forehead, and she kept her eyes trained on the lilac blossoms of a Pride of India which was growing in the lane so that her emotions weren't so on view.

'I think she was just unhappy,' she explained tentatively then. 'Domesticity got to her, I guess, and so as soon as I left school she found herself a high-flying job and then just seemed to lose interest in Dad and me. Three months later she'd gone. I suppose she suddenly found freedom—independence,' she palliated, with a small shrug, 'and wanted a career and a more satisfying life to make up for the years she'd spent just being a housewife.' But she didn't tell him everything, somehow unable to bring herself to do so, finishing with a rueful little sigh, 'Dad sold the house soon afterwards and brought me to the States to try and make a new life for us there.'

'And then he died?' It wasn't a clever guess. Madeline had told him the basic facts about her eight years ago—plus a lot that weren't true, Lee reflected bitterly. She nodded.

'So how did you come to meet my father?'

She stiffened, meeting the hard demand of his question with a nervous tightening of her throat. So that was why he had brought her here. An interrogation on the road wasn't good for concentration, plus there had been, of course, the added inconvenience of traffic jams and Gombey dancers. He wanted her alone, and he knew as well as she did that Alec was due back at the house any time now.

Uneasily, she moistened her dry lips. 'He sort of knew Dad because Dad had spent some time in New York years ago,' she started to explain somewhat astringently, 'and they met up again when we emigrated. Anyway, they arranged it that if anything happened to Dad, Richard would take me in. But I didn't move in with him to be his mistress,' she said emphatically, meeting a flickering density in those dark irises that made her stomach muscles contract.

'And you're saying the situation didn't develop?'

Colour winged its way upwards across her cheeks. 'Yes, that's exactly what I'm saying!'

'Then why didn't you put up more opposition against my deductions eight years ago, Coralie? If I remember rightly, you seemed to go out of your way before you left that house to convince me that those rumours were right. If you're so innocent, why the hell didn't you try harder to convince me of it then?'

Leaning with his elbow on his thigh, chin resting on his fist, there was a threat in every dominant inch of him. His gaze, too, was dark with accusation, but nevertheless Lee managed to hold it levelly.

'Would you have listened?' she challenged poignantly.

He didn't need to answer that.

'Anyway, I was rather outnumbered,' she reminded him bitterly, remembering how Madeline had lied. And with wounded accusation, she added, 'You'd never have taken my word against hers.'

His mouth quirked, the firm lower lip suggestive of a passion she was trying not to think about, and, uncomfortably, she shifted her gaze from the raw intensity of his.

'It wasn't only what Madeline said.' Briefly, that gaze flitted over the tenuous lines of her body, down over her breasts and the accentuated curve of her hips. 'You weren't exactly the type even then that a man would have wanted to stop simply at playing guardian to,' he surprised her by saying after the way he'd mocked her gawky young body at the time. 'And my father was certainly no saint! Besides, a man doesn't usually open his house to an attractive girl, and then leave her all his money,' he remarked with hard scepticism, 'unless she's been that. . .special to him.'

Which was what everyone had said.

'Well, I wasn't!' Anger flaring, she dumped her half-empty mug down on the table and got up, crossing over to the fireplace. 'And if you'd called to see him a bit more, instead of being so tied up with your own life, you might have been more entitled to make judgements about the relationship. . .seen how *special* I was!'

For a moment his eyes glittered with some dark emotion that seemed to stretch the skin tight over his cheekbones. Then it was gone, and in its place was a parody of a smile that didn't go beyond his lips.

'Is that what my father told you?' he said quietly, getting up. 'That I was "tied up" with my life?'

'No,' she admitted, looking at him broodily from under her lashes, thinking how much that hard masculinity imposed in the tiny room. 'He didn't say very much about you at all, but he must have thought it. I lived with him for the best part of four months, and you didn't come to see him once,' she went on, feeling for the older man. 'I know you were abroad at the time, but in view of his state of health, I would have thought you could have dragged yourself away from whatever important business you had to see him sometimes.'

She licked her lips, guessing she'd been too outspoken as she sensed the tangible anger in him.

'Now who's making judgements?' he breathed with a soft reprehension, moving towards her with an intimidating purposefulness that made Lee swallow hard. 'Hadn't it occurred to you, my sweet, innocent child, that I stayed away from my father not because I had more important things to do, as you put it, but because he wanted me to? Surely he must have mentioned *that*?

Or was he so determined to protect you from the sordid realities of life that he kept that from you as well?'

His tongue flayed, and Lee bit her bottom lip, trying to ignore how devastating he looked in anger, wondering, at the same time, what he meant. Richard, though, she remembered, had seldom talked about his son, and, for all his kindness, hadn't been the type of man to invite questions of any kind—or one that she could easily get close to.

Even so, she was surprised when she heard Jordan say, 'We simply never got on. Not from when I was a child till the day I joined him in his business. We could never agree on a thing. But, for all that, he *was* my father and therefore very special to me.' The admonishment was unmistakable, a hard, shaming rebuke for challenging him as she had just now. 'I don't suppose it means a darn thing to you,' he went on with an odd intensity in his voice, 'but I admired him in many ways. I didn't want an estrangement from him. I would have given the world to have prevented it. But there were. . .' he hesitated '. . .differences of opinion. Oh, it's a far too complicated story to go into.' He sighed heavily. 'But since you raised the subject, *he* cut *me* out of his life. I was the one who wanted to bridge the chasm, but he wouldn't soften. I don't know why— whether it was his pride, the generation gap, or just plain hatred for me, but he wouldn't see me for the last eighteen months of his life. I didn't hear a thing from him until I received that cable from Madeline.' And in a tone suddenly raw with emotion, 'He didn't even tell me he was. . .'

He struck the stonework of the fireplace as though to rid himself of some of the anguish that had roughened his voice, lined the arresting symmetry of his features, and, watching him, Lee felt her heart twist inside of her. Naïve as she had been, she had never entertained the thought that he might have been so totally estranged from his father—let alone not known that he was ill. But no one had said anything to her, and she had been too young and immersed in her own misery to recognise that dark grief in him as anything more than just natural mourning. But what did that legacy make her in view of the relationship between Jordan and his father? she wondered suddenly. Hardly anything else, surely, but a symbol of his father's contempt for him?

A cold emptiness spread through her as she began to see her inheritance for just what it was, but that inner agony she had sensed in Jordan opened up everything that was instinctively feminine in her.

Heedlessly, she moved to slide her hand over his, a pale, slender sculpture against the dark strength of bronze.

'I'm sorry,' she whispered, thinking how futile that sounded. 'I really am.' After all, hadn't she known what it felt like to be shunned by a parent? Known the soul-searching agony—the guilt—that perhaps it might be all one's own fault?

'Are you?' he said quietly, looking at her with such a pained question in his eyes that her heart felt as if it were melting, so that when his fingers opened and closed again, trapping hers with their impervious strength, she didn't even try to pull away. 'You know, for all these years I've thought that if our paths ever crossed again, I'd happily strangle you. And now. . .' Hard, questioning doubt burned in the wounded darkness of his eyes, vying with a raw, basic hunger that sent a reckless excitement shivering through her blood.

'And now?' she queried shakily.

He didn't answer, but caught her to him with a rough

possessiveness, the hand in her hair tugging her head back for the hard acceptance of his mouth. His passion was pulsing and feverish, the hard demands of his desire dragging breath from his lungs, from hers, so that she was panting as he rained urgent kisses over her face and neck, groaned heavily against her hair, 'For heaven's sake, convince me, Coralie!'

His mouth on hers again ignited a fire deep down inside of her, an elemental need of him that sent twinges of desire arrowing through her loins. He was seeking solace in the pure femininity of her, and she wanted to give it—take away his pain—but more desperately, make him believe the truth about her, and in the only way she could.

Sensations coursed through her, an intensifying hunger that was fed by the urgency of his hands moving over her back and buttocks and the smooth curve of her hips—sliding her dress up so that she felt their tantalising warmth against her bare thighs. The roughness of his jaw where he hadn't shaved since that morning, grazed hers, the deepening intimacy of his kiss demanding and conquering, so that when he lifted her over to the settee and sat down with her across his lap, she was too languid with desire to protest, even if she'd wanted to.

Every sense was imbued with him, his scent, his warmth, his hardness, the slightly salty taste of his skin, every feminine cell crying out for the mate it knew it wanted, as he dealt deftly with the buttons of her dress and pushed aside the thin material to caress the aching roundness of her breasts. His touch elicited a small, broken sob from her, and she felt the dark peaks responding like flowers beneath the warm stimulus of the sun. He groaned his appreciation, his lips warm as they caressed the scar on her temple, the sweet torture of his hands extending to the smooth line of her rib-cage and tiny waist, moving with a gentle pressure over the flat plane of her abdomen. Desire held her in thrall, her fingers twisting in the thin fabric of his shirt, fire licking along her veins as his hand slipped beneath the thin lace of her briefs to trace the silken pathway of her loins, finding with a sighed satisfaction the moist warmth of her femininity.

She shuddered her response, her breath catching in her lungs. She had never known it could be like this. Men's advances to her, as far as she had allowed, had been purely self-gratifying and clumsy, not this subtle, exquisite pleasure that robbed her of everything but a craving to give and give and give. . .

'No, Coralie. Not here. Not now.'

His gentle recommendation brought her eyes flickering open—dark and tortured in her softly flushed face—her hair tumbling like black silk across his arm. The gaze that locked with hers burned with a fierce and mutual hunger for her, the colour across the tanned skin and the tautness of his mouth and jaw evident of a driving passion he was doing his utmost to control.

Outside, a shower had gone unnoticed with the patter of raindrops against the pane. But now a ray of sunshine broke through the late afternoon cloud, spilling like liquid gold across her face and the smooth satin of her breasts, and she heard Jordan say huskily, 'You're beautiful.'

Aching with need, she uttered a small, frustrated sound, reaching to caress his strong cheek with the back of her hand. Then, drawing courage from the knowledge of his own need of her, she explored the warm curve of his shoulder beneath his shirt, her aching fingers, hungry for more of him, acquainting themselves with the solid wall of his chest, the velvet of his lean waist, that wiry texture of dark hair arrowing its way past his belt. . .

She closed her eyes, losing the courage to look at him as she sought the ultimate intimacy—the experience new to her—her fingers against the dark fabric, trembling and unsure. He made a hoarse sound, catching her hand so hard that she thought she had angered him. But then, with a groan of defeat he was moving across her, trapping her between the soft, yielding cushions and the muscular strength of his torso, so that then he was the one in command, his lips and hands demanding until she moved against him like a frenzied animal.

She wanted to know him completely—intimately—a man she'd known for so short a time, yet whom she knew was hers—had been hers, in spite of everything, all those years ago. And she didn't know why she thought that. Only that she wanted him as a friend, and, almost desperately, as her lover—knew instinctively now, as she offered him the secret treasure of her body, that she would never, ever want anyone else. . .

He helped her wriggle out of the rest of her clothes, and removed his own with such economy of timing that she scarcely knew he had until the heated velvet of his skin touched hers. And then she was his, alive only to his lips and his tongue and his hands, and the sudden, agonising pain that wrung a stifled cry from her lips. But the pain was swift, leaving only a blinding, driving ecstasy as he took her with him, higher and higher into a spinning orbit of sensation, a union that assuaged the endless years of waiting—the unconscious knowledge that she had been created to submit solely to this man—and at the moment when his soul poured into her, it was like being made whole, a fusing of two halves, like coming home.

For an eternity she lay quite still beneath him, slumbrous from the aftermath of their lovemaking. Her face turned against his shoulder, she listened to the deep, steady sound of his breathing, the passion that had ravaged her senses replaced by a sweet, exquisite tenderness that filled her with a glowing warmth. Then she gave a little murmur, as his weight became too much to take.

He eased himself up and she could feel his intent scrutiny even through her closed lids. She smiled wantonly—languorously—up at him, and without opening her eyes lifted her mouth for his kiss. But instead he said with soft, repressed anger, 'Why the hell didn't you tell me—stop me?'

Her eyes flickered open, questioning the berating note in his voice, his sudden withdrawal from her leaving her with a feeling of immense loss.

'Because I didn't want to,' she murmured, hurt—baffled—by his obvious displeasure. 'Anyway, what difference does it make?'

He moved away from her and swiftly began dressing. 'I would have thought it made every difference in the world.' An eyebrow lifted chasteningly as he shot a glance her way. 'Particularly to you. In my experience, a woman doesn't reach twenty-five and still keep her virginity without it meaning something to her. So why me, Coralie?'

Because I love you, came her unchecked, yet indisputable response—surprising even herself—but silently, achingly, because he was looking at her with such dark censure in his eyes that she was beginning to feel ashamed. Quickly, she followed his example and began pulling on her clothes, aware of him tucking his shirt into the waistband of his trousers—anger reflected in his movements—and tremulously she uttered, 'Why are you so annoyed? Most men would be delighted to discover they'd been the first.'

'Well, I'm not most men.' The powerful muscles moved beneath the soft shirt as he stood there, hands splayed against his lean hips, looking down at her. 'I shouldn't think a lot of men would give a damn,' he said roughly. 'But I do. And I've been around long enough to realise that virgins don't have affairs. So why with me?'

So that was it. He hadn't intended to make love to her at all, but in doing so must have assumed—even if he'd accepted the truth about her and his father—that her experience went some way to matching his own. But he'd been proved wrong, and so had she, she thought with heart-rending anguish, in being so naïve as to imagine that he'd felt the same overpowering oneness with her as she'd felt with him, that his lovemaking was anything other than a casual, pleasurable experience with a willing partner.

Bitter tears stung her eyes, and, fighting to keep them from him—from allowing him to guess at her foolish emotions—she said, far more nonchalantly than she could help, 'Why not with you? Every virgin has to start somewhere. And I don't see why you should mind, unless you can't stand concrete proof that you've been wrong about me all along.'

As soon as she said it, she wished she hadn't, but it was too late, and she recoiled from the hard, flaying question that was suddenly burning in Jordan's eyes.

'Is that all this was?' His jaw jerked roughly towards the settee, that narrowed gaze running almost contemptuously over her semi-nakedness. 'Just a means of gleaning some warped satisfaction out of proving me wrong?'

'Of course not, I——'

'And have you given any consideration at all to contraception?' It was a harsh demand, cutting through her attempted denial of his accusation. 'Is there the remotest chance that I could have just made you pregnant?'

His words were scathing, burning across her heart like cruel flames. She had made love with him because she had wanted him—not just with her body, but with her soul—and any consequences resulting from her actions hadn't entered her mind, although Jordan must have naturally assumed she was taking precautions.

Too ashamed to openly admit that she could easily be carrying his child, stiffly, with a pressure on her windpipe, she said, 'Don't worry, Jordan. I shan't slap a paternity suit on you, if that's all you're concerned about. I'm quite capable of providing on my own for any child I might conceive.'

'I'm sure you are.' His dry, clipped comment made her wonder if he was remembering just how much money his father had left her, the reminder stinging, before he said quietly, 'But there's just one thing you've forgotten. It would be my child, too.'

'Would that bother you?'

He caught his breath. Then, 'Yes. It just so happens that it would.'

She looked at him quickly, at the proud, strong angles of his face, realising he was a man of integrity, and shame burned through her with the pain that was eating at her heart. He would never have been so reckless and impetuous as to risk conceiving an unwanted child, even in a love relationship, she realised self-reproachfully; and, making love with her certainly hadn't been, she had to accept, injurious though it was. He would never have been so angry with her if it had been. And the fact that she loved him—would have welcomed a child from him, had he loved her—didn't make her stupidity any more excusable.

He didn't say a word to her on the journey back, and when he deliberately avoided her by skipping dinner—burying himself in his uncle's study—she knew she couldn't stay in Bermuda any longer. Therefore, the following day, a phone call from her secretary advising of further problems with the magazine gave her the excuse she sorely needed to get away. The thought of leaving Jordan tore at her heart, but his cold indifference towards her hurt more, and she knew that if she stayed she would run the risk of his finding out how much he meant to her, and she couldn't bear the humiliation of that. Consequently, after making her apologies to Alec—managing to convince him that she was desperately needed in New York—she packed her suitcase and, that very afternoon, flew home.

CHAPTER EIGHT

'Why don't you just put yourself out of your misery and have an affair with him?'

Lee glanced up from her desk to see Vince standing in the doorway, studying her rather too sagaciously.

'Who?' she asked, pretending not to know, and avoided looking at him as he came in by ferreting for some papers under the disorganised mountain of correspondence that had accumulated since she had been away. She would really have to teach Rachael to be tidier!

'You know very well. That Colyer guy.'

She flinched at the name, but hid it well, determined that Vince wouldn't know how she was feeling.

'Oh, him,' she uttered with forced casualness, and, finding the elusive notes under a file, dragged them towards her. 'What makes you think I'd want an affair with *him*? Anyway, I don't know what you're getting at,' she bluffed—though with an unexpected tremor she couldn't control—and, sending a glance towards her friend's blond, rangy figure, added, 'I'm not miserable.'

'No?' There was no mistaking the scepticism in the Cockney tones as the photographer came round and perched himself on the corner of her desk. 'I don't think there's a soul in this building who'd care to lay bets on that, me ol' love. More than one person has noticed that you haven't been yourself since you got back, and Rachael tells me you're skipping meals. Besides, you've got that "he doesn't want to marry me,

131

but he wants me to be more than just a friend" look. I know. I've seen it many times before.'

'Yes, probably on the face of every girl you've dated!' Lee remonstrated, trying for a smile to hide the aching void inside her, her dark hair framing a face that was softly golden from the Bermuda sun.

'Now, that isn't fair.' Vince gave her a lopsided look, one denim-clad leg dangling. 'You know I'm not the slippers and armchair type—that I don't like being tied to one situation for too long—but you. . .' He leaned towards her, his blue eyes unusually concerned. 'You'll stick at one thing and see it through to the bitter end if you think it will work, because you're like that, Lee, which probably means you're also a one-man woman—the type that gets hurt. Only a fool wouldn't be able to see that something happened to you in Bermuda, and with a guy like Colyer around, it doesn't take much working out. And I was only kidding, incidentally, about you having an affair with him.' Lee detected the hint of a warning in his voice. 'He's totally irresistible to women, and I can see why, but hardly the type to cut your teeth on. And with his reputation with the opposite sex, and your lack of one. . .' He made an expressive gesture with his hands. 'With a man like that, kiddo, you play the game by his rules, or you don't play at all.'

Lee flinched from the truth of his words, and wondered what Vince would say if she told him that she had already discovered that; that it was Jordan's incensed reaction when he'd discovered she was a virgin—coupled with her shame over the way she'd made an utter fool of herself with him—that had brought her back from Bermuda earlier than she had intended, because, quite simply, she had turned tail and run. And what hurt most was that Jordan had let her, without a flicker of emotion, driving her to the airport that day without so much as even a murmur of wanting to see her again, and she could only assume, from his cool, forced courtesy towards her on that journey, that he'd been relieved to see her go. After all, what had there been on his part but a mere physical attraction? A desire for sexual conquest, which had been replaced by anger when that desire had been realised and he'd found out that he was the first? And why he'd been so angry, she wasn't sure, unless he truly believed she'd wanted to make a fool of him— make him feel guilty for thinking what he had about her for all those years. But whatever the reason, she meditated painfully, it didn't spring from his undying devotion to her, while stupidly, she had allowed herself to become emotionally involved with him.

And that was an understatement, she accepted unwillingly now, because, short though their acquaintance had been, she was desperately in love with him. At first she had wanted to blame the magic of Bermuda, tried calling this hopeless, futile emotion the result of a holiday affair, hoping that the pain would gradually ease with the fading of her sun-tan. But it hadn't. And only now, for the first time since she'd been back, could she fully admit to herself that her feelings stretched far beyond the boundaries of any holiday romance. People fell in love on a first meeting. After a week or a year. There were no rules laid down for the length of time it took to lose one's heart to someone. She had just happened to do so in less than two weeks, and with a man who, thankfully, didn't have the slightest inkling of it. And the only consolation to be gleaned from her stupid folly was that she hadn't become pregnant because of it.

'Don't worry,' she said lightly. 'I won't be seeing him

again.' But her eyes mirrored the pain inside her, and she saw the understanding look Vince gave her as he deposited some photographs on her desk before sliding off.

'There's always me, darlin',' he smiled sympathetically from the doorway—long arms outstretched beneath his khaki shirt—and the sad thing was that she knew he meant it.

'Get out,' she flung back at him affectionately, a piece of screwed-up paper finding its goal in the middle of his lean chest. 'I've got more important things to worry about, like whether or not we'll all have jobs this time next month.'

Now that she was back, the problems with the magazine had come crowding in around her again, although in some way she was almost grateful for them, as they helped to keep her mind off Jordan. Since returning to the office six weeks ago she hadn't had a moment to herself, and certainly no time to dwell on personal problems. *Eve's Apple*, for everyone's efforts, was facing a very gloomy future, and it was taking every ounce of ingenuity and energy Lee could summon up to convince the other directors of the company that it still had one!

And she was made to face further reality of it as Rachael suddenly came rushing in, almost colliding with Vince.

'Bad news, I'm afraid, Lee,' she burst out rather breathlessly, a mass of unruly red hair clashing with her hot, flushed cheeks. 'I've just had Sales on, and they tell me we've lost Harbingers to some other mag. How could they do that?' she wailed, glancing up at Vince who was leaning against the door-jamb, looking as dismayed as the two women. When things went wrong, they all took it personally, Lee realised, feeling sick inside. Harbingers had been with them since the beginning. 'They've been advertising with us since we started!' Rachael moaned again, echoing Lee's thoughts. 'How could they do that to us?'

'They can and they have,' Lee accepted, calm on the outside, although inwardly she was beginning to despair. It was happening too often these days. Clients pulling out, advised by their agencies, perhaps, that *Eve's Apple* wasn't such a rosy-looking outlet any more. 'We've just got to win them back, that's all,' she said determinedly then, thrusting out her chin in a way the other two knew meant business. 'Them. Others we've lost. Plus as many new accounts as we can possibly get. And that means sales. And we all know what that means, don't we?' Her eyes flashed a challenge at Rachael and Vince, as though the two of them alone were responsible for the journal's future. 'It means good articles. Good pictures. And an overall confidence to show these ad agencies that we're not going to be squeezed out of the market place.' Which were optimistic words, she thought unhappily when she was on her own again, because deep down she felt that they were fighting a losing battle. The magazine needed money, and already the company's borrowing limit had been well-exceeded. The bank weren't lending any more, a fact confirmed by the company's accountant at a directors' meeting the following day.

'Things aren't good, Lee,' he hit her with as soon as she walked into the small boardroom, the only corner of the building that wasn't under siege by time-pressed journalists, ringing telephones and clattering machines. 'As the major shareholder, of course, you've got the final say,' he reminded her solemnly from behind his rimless spectacles, 'and I know it's tougher for you than anyone else, as *Eve's Apple* was your baby, but if things don't pick up within, say. . .the next six to eight weeks. . .my advice unquestionably is that you sell out. I know of one or two companies who might be interested and——'

'Which means it's still a viable proposition!' Lee cut in trenchantly. 'Otherwise they wouldn't even consider it. In which case, it's rather defeatist of us even thinking about selling out.' She looked at the other directors around the table: Peter Whiteside from Advertising, Marjorie Tugstall from Editorial, and Clive Hunnicut from Circulation and Accounts. 'If another company can make it work, then surely we can? It's just a question of pulling our belts in for a while, and working to a very strict budget.'

'And relying on some of that enthusiasm of yours to pay our salaries,' Clive said drily, massaging a neatly trimmed beard.

The sarcasm hurt, but Lee couldn't blame him for feeling the way he did. He was worried—as they all were—and both Clive and Peter had young families to support. But she couldn't sell out. She couldn't!

'What we *need* is a few leading stories like this one,' Marjorie stressed, fingering the new month's publication which contained the first instalment of the feature on Alec Mason. 'You really excelled with this one, Lee.' Marjorie was forty plus, and a brilliant editor, and such a stickler for perfection, it was rumoured she'd been born with a blue pencil in her hand. 'It's dynamic!' she breathed in her usual dramatic manner, her face glowing with appreciation of her younger colleague's work. 'What were you driven by out there? Some hidden source of inspiration?'

'What, blushes?' was the young ad director's too shrewd observation. 'Perhaps our Chief Pip's met a tall, dark potential husband in Bermuda. If so, I only hope he's rich.'

She couldn't bear it, but she had to, passing off their remarks with an indulgent, and somewhat forced, smile. But alone in her office, looking through her copy of the magazine, bitter-sweet memories of Bermuda leaped up from each page she turned; in the softly rolling landscape, in the sunny lighthouse, in the opalescent waters of the Great Sound. A far cry from New York and the rather dull June morning, she thought torturedly, finding it all too painful a reminder that she'd been talking with Jordan while those photographs were being taken. Respect for him had been born in her that day, she remembered with rueful longing—and how reluctant she had been then to acknowledge it! If only she had been able to maintain her resistance—refused to submit to that dark, hidden chemistry that had attracted her to him as recklessly as a cliff edge attracted a lemming. Instead of which she had totally ignored the danger signs, and plunged head over heels in love with him!

And to add to all her other problems the car started playing up.

'It's going to be a big job,' the mechanic told her, when she took it in to her usual garage that evening. Resignedly, he slammed down the bonnet of her small green saloon. 'I'm afraid I can't do anything with it tonight. If you'd like to leave it, I'll try and start work on it first thing tomorrow morning, and I recommend that you do. I don't think it's safe to drive anywhere at the moment.'

Lee's heart sank. Tonight didn't particularly matter. It was her birthday and Vince had persuaded her to go out for a pizza with him and Rachael and several others from the office, and she could get a cab to the restaurant. But tomorrow she had two important appointments out of town, and no car could well mean the loss of two very important clients she was doing her utmost to hang on to.

'You don't have anything I could hire, do you?' she asked the man rather dejectedly, glancing around at several cars standing idly behind the workshop.

'Only Mick's,' the man stated, tossing a glance over his shoulder at a gleaming Jaguar sports car. 'He's in Los Angeles at the moment, and won't be needing it for three or four days, but he never minds you borrowing his cars, as you know.'

Mick was the proprietor, and a friend, and was always keen to help her out, and now Lee grasped at the offer without hesitation.

The sky threatened rain as she pulled into the basement of the apartment block. More like November than Midsummer's Day, she thought with a mental grimace, carefully manoeuvring the expensive car into her parking space.

She heard a car door slam as she was locking her own, then the soft tread of footsteps, and she tensed, every nerve suddenly alert. Since the mugging in Bermuda she had become unduly nervous in lonely places, and the car park was lonelier than most. Fear lifted the hairs on the back of her neck as she turned, letting out a small, strangled cry as a man suddenly emerged from behind a pillar.

Fear, both sick and chilling, was chased away by relief and, as quickly, shock.

'I'm sorry. I didn't mean to frighten you,' Contrition laced the deep Canadian tones which were washing over her like a breath-catching wave.

In a dark, well-cut business suit, Jordan Colyer

projected an image of the high-powered, successful male—that raw, omnipotent magnetism so overwhelming her that she placed a steadying hand on the Jaguar, weak from too many emotions to cope with all at once.

'What brings you here?' She sounded—felt!—as if she had just run a mile.

'You.' The dark sweep of his lashes concealed some indefinable emotion as his eyes followed the give-away gesture of her hand, and Lee moistened her top lip, warmth tingling through her. Of course. It was a rather stupid question. Why else would he be in her car park? Under her apartment block?

'Things going well?' His gaze embraced the car.

'Oh, this!' Red-tipped fingers ran reverently over the bonnet, and she gave a nervous little laugh. 'It's only hired.'

'Only?' He grimaced, obviously deciding that she definitely had to be doing well—not realising that she hadn't paid a cent for the privilege of borrowing the Jag—and she decided to keep him believing it. For her pride's sake, she didn't want him knowing how bad things really were.

'Are you coming up?' she invited, with the smallest hint of a tremor.

A smile tugged at the corner of his mouth, the familiar, engaging gesture causing Lee's heart to lurch. 'I thought you'd never ask.'

His gaze raked over her as the lift ascended to her floor, a hand in his trouser pocket as he made an uncomfortably blatant survey of her rather too slender figure pressed against the opposite wall. With slow speculation, his eyes took in the tanned satin of her skin, the wide curve of her mouth and the dark shadows beneath her eyes which were somehow emphasised by the pristine whiteness of a fashionably casual suit, and that commanding mouth pulled down hard.

'You look tired,' he reprehended softly, noticing everything, as always. 'Are you. . .all right?' The hesitation in his voice spoke volumes.

Sticking out her chin, Lee said rather bluntly, 'I'm not pregnant, if that's what you mean.'

She wasn't sure if that was relief in his eyes, but she heard him catch his breath.

'Yes, that's exactly what I meant,' he said raggedly. 'So how do you account for looking rather peaky, and as if you've lost a pound or two more than is entirely advisable?'

Because I haven't been able to eat or sleep properly because of you! her heart cried achingly, but casually enough she responded, 'Things have been rather hectic these days.' Then swiftly changed the subject by asking, 'How's Alec?'

'Fine.'

'And Arlene?'

It was polite, constrained conversation—on both their parts, she felt. That mutual attraction, which had flared like a forest fire in Bermuda, lay like a bed of hot embers between them now, an incandescent heat that, despite past hostilities—perhaps even because of them—waited for one careless sigh to fan the flames. She was glad when the lift doors opened and she was letting him into her airy, less confining apartment.

'Coffee?'

'Please.'

When she came back with the tray, he was sitting on one of the easy chairs, browsing, almost interestedly, through a past issue of her magazine. He laid it aside and stood up as soon as he saw her.

'If you hadn't heard—they caught your mugger. Or

rather, he confessed,' he informed her softly, as if he appreciated how the memory of that night still gave her nightmares sometimes, and he smiled at her surprise. 'However, I didn't come here just to tell you that. I wanted you to know what a marvellous job you made of the story on Alec,' he complimented, watching her set the tray down on the small, yew coffee-table, which matched a bookcase and a hi-fi cabinet on the other side of the room. 'I was very impressed. It also provided me with a darn good excuse to see you again.'

She met the probing intensity of his gaze with her heart starting to race—her legs weakening. Why? Why had he wanted to see her? she wondered, with a sudden raging optimism.

'I was angry with you that last day. . .' he started to explain to the misty aquamarine eyes that questioned his '. . .after we——' He broke off, thrust his hands into his pockets and swung away to the balcony window, startling a small bird from the seed-dispenser Lee had bought in Hamilton that day, his gaze following its flight down across the leafy green mantle of New York's Central Park. The fine cut of his suit emphasised the superb power of his shoulders and long legs, the memory of that naked strength against her causing the unwelcome clutch of desire to tighten in her loins.

'I was angry with myself—not you,' he was saying with surprising softness as he turned around, the unexpected admission, with the hard, masculine beauty of his features, taking her breath away. 'It was pretty tough being hit with the knowledge that you were a virgin, when I was still trying—*wanting*,' he accentuated strongly, 'to accept that I'd been wrong about the sort of girl I'd believed you were.'

'But you accused me of getting some sort of warped

satisfaction out of it,' Lee reminded him, baffled, toying absently with the buttons of her jacket.

'Yes, I know,' he accepted drily, 'but I didn't fully believe that, although I couldn't really have blamed you if you had. I have to confess I was trying to appease my own guilt about thinking so badly about you for so long—as well as not giving any consideration to the slender chance that there might not have been anyone else.' He shrugged, moving away from the window, filling her starved senses with that subtle, unforgettable fragrance of his cologne. 'I never find it easy admitting I've been wrong, Coralie,' he told her with glaring truthfulness, his mouth pulling down in self-deprecation. 'I'm afraid it's a family trait.' Something in those darkening eyes made her guess that he was thinking about his father, and her heart gave a little twist for him. 'All I can ask of you is that you accept my apologies, and to suggest that we might perhaps start again. . .at the beginning.'

'I'd like that,' Lee murmured tentatively, her eyes trained on his as though she were half afraid he might disappear if she looked away. Her heart suddenly full, she wanted him to come across and take her in his arms, even though she knew she'd be completely out of control if he did.

And perhaps he knew it, too, because he didn't— stooping to pick something up from the chair he'd been sitting in, before moving with that lithe, animal grace of his towards her.

'Another reason for my coming here this evening was to give you this.'

Surprised, Lee took the small, square package he handed to her. It was heavy—very heavy for its size, she thought curiously, starting to undo the pretty silver wrapping.

A little gasp left her as she removed his gift carefully from its box. It was a paperweight, the cold, clear glass cleverly cut into the perfect shape of an apple. Inside though, a myriad of delicate, icelike shapes hinted at doves and flowers, and in the centre, a filigreed, fountainlike spray of crystal—an almost abstract representation of some imagined Utopia that brought a lump to Lee's throat and, unexpectedly, tears to her eyes.

'Happy Birthday, little Eve.'

The deep voice brought her head up, her face revealing every one of the emotions which were pulsing through her. How had he known?

He looked smug, she thought, those perfect lineaments moulded in satisfaction at her obvious pleasure. Vaguely, then, she recalled casually mentioning her birthday to him the day he'd asked her about her necklace. Not only had he remembered, though, he'd obviously gone out of his way to provide something that was entirely unique. Too unique to have been acquired by chance, she realised, gazing down at the miniature Eden. He'd had it made especially for her, she knew without even having to ask him, just as she knew that, with that inherent, artistic streak of his, it would have been to his own design.

'It's beautiful,' she whispered.

'So are you.'

She looked up at him, the sensual velvet of his voice sending that familiar excitement quivering through her. And, as if he knew, he was taking the small gift and putting it down on the table—pulling her into his arms.

'For heaven's sake, I can't keep this up any longer!' he rasped, before his mouth covered hers—hungrily, desperately—her own response to it total and uninhibited, because she was soaking in the life-force of his passion like a parched and thirsty desert needing rain.

They were both breathing raggedly as he left her mouth, only to clasp her to him, his embrace so hard and unyielding, it almost hurt. The fabric of his suit was coolly sensual against her cheek, which, with his male scent and the hard warmth of him, was driving everything but her need for him from her mind.

Oh, I love you! She had to bite her lip to stop herself uttering it aloud, afraid that such a rash declaration might send him away again, because he hadn't actually mentioned anything about love. But when his mouth closed over hers again she couldn't so easily hide the precipitous demands of her body. It was like an addiction—this need of him, his kiss—the drug she craved, the moist warmth of his mouth on hers at first satisfying and then not enough, the small murmur that escaped her when his hands found the swelling fullness of her breasts a plea for a greater stimulation. She was aching for him, fire surging through her loins, the way she ground her hips sensuously against his a flagrant appeal to him that seemed to snap whatever control he had and had him sweeping her up into his arms.

'Where's the bedroom?'

She couldn't answer—too breathless to speak—but he found it easily enough, dropping down with her on to the bed. The hard reality of him after the weeks of futile longing brought her straining towards him, hungry for the mouth that seemed suddenly to be devouring her, the hands that were tugging mercilessly at her clothes.

'Oh, my beautiful, beautiful girl. . .I want you.'

She heard his ragged words through a sensual delirium, unaware that her own fingers were fumbling tremblingly with the buttons of his shirt. Somehow, within seconds, she was naked and so was he, a small gasp escaping her as she felt the familiar warm strength of him against her, the heated dampness of his skin meet and cling sensuously to hers. She moved like some uninhibited wanton as his lips and hands rediscovered her, hearing her own small sobs like a stranger's voice, her tongue, against the crisp hair of his chest, tasting the slight saltiness of his skin, her flaring nostrils greedy for the raw, animal scent of him.

His lips were urgent against her soft warmth, anointing her breasts, her waist, her loins, his hard breathing revealing the extreme restraint he was exercising over his own passion, while his mouth marked an insidious trail of pleasure down across her body to the aching sweetness of her femininity.

'No!' Needles of desire pierced her like spears of sweet agony, her deep, shuddering protest springing from a need too intense for anything but his ultimate possession. And he seemed to know the demands of her body as well as he knew his own, moving above her and taking her then with a hard, driving urgency that carried them both to the very pinnacle of ecstasy, sensation meeting sensation in a shattering climax of mutual release that had them collapsing together, damp and breathless, in a sweet, welcoming lethargy of fulfilment.

A long time later she said quietly, 'You came prepared, didn't you?' Because, in spite of his overpowering passion, he'd spared enough thought to protect her this time from becoming pregnant. Though she was grateful for that, she couldn't help considering, a little woundedly, how sure he must have been of her continuing weakness for him, wondered even if he'd guessed it would take him less than half an hour to get her into bed.

He was raising himself up on his elbows, dark eyes raking over her, tender and warm. 'Well, one of us had

to be,' he advised gently, smiling as he pushed back
the tendrils of her damp hair. 'Would you rather I
hadn't?'

No, of course she wouldn't. 'I just don't like feeling
that you'd guessed I'd be so easy,' she murmured, hurt,
and heard him laugh quietly in his throat.

'I'm sorry,' he whispered, his voice deep and sincere,
the lips against her temple suddenly shocking her into
acknowledging a desire only minutes ago she had
thought sated. 'I didn't intend it to happen, either.' He
pulled a wry face. 'Well, not quite like this. But when
I'm with you I lose all sense of responsibility, and as
much as the thought of making you pregnant excites
me, I'd rather it didn't happen simply because I lost
control. And if anyone's made an easy conquest. . .'
he kissed her very gently on the mouth—gave a small
groan from the wanting inside of him '. . .it's you over
me, little Eve.' His mouth was warm against her throat,
her shoulder, and she felt the peaks of her breasts grow
taut, recognised that familiar tingling in her loins, and
realised, with a quickening of her pulse, the extent of
his own new arousal. With a lover's skill he was making
her want him again, dispelling the foolish little doubts
that had plagued her for a few moments because of
something Vince had said. . .

She shot up in bed. 'Oh, good grief! I had a date!'

'*What?*' Swiftly, Jordan was sitting up beside her.
'Who with?' he demanded, eyes narrowing.

He looked so grim that a little bubble of amusement
escaped her. 'Only with a couple of friends from the
office,' she enlightened, smiling, happier now. 'But I'd
better call Vince and explain. You remember
Vince. . .'

Some emotion played across the strong mould of his
face and his lips compressed. 'Yes,' he breathed,

deliberately unenamoured, as Lee slid out of his arms and pulled on a robe. Obviously, he still had doubts about her relationship with the photographer, she realised, because there was a branding heat about those eyes that watched from the bed as she made the call, a hard possessiveness that sent a small thrill through her in realising that he was jealous.

'I'm afraid I can't make it tonight,' she explained to the disembodied voice at the other end of the line. 'Something's come up. I'm sorry.'

'It wouldn't be six foot plus and fresh out of the Bermuda Triangle, would it?' was Vince's dry remark.

Tremulously, Lee laughed, but said as nonchalantly as she could, 'How did you guess?' hoping that Jordan hadn't detected that breathless quality to her voice, that sighing in her blood that might make him realise just how much she was in love with him.

'That's great. I'm pleased for you. But be careful, ol' love. Rumour has it that man's got a ruthless streak a mile wide. Just don't get hurt, will you?'

'Thanks for the advice,' she returned, but somewhat frostily, because she didn't want to listen to any more rumours about Jordan. Of course a man like him would attract gossip. Someone as successful and attractive as he was always did. But she loved him. And she fully believed that, given time, she could make him love her—a hope that burned in her over the ensuing weeks with her intensifying feelings for him which, somehow, still unsure of him, she managed to keep closely guarded from him—even in bed.

And they made love often—like desperate, guilty lovers who couldn't get enough of each other—on the tiny bed in her modest apartment, or in the more sumptuous, penthouse luxury of his.

He was a solicitous lover, sometimes turning up at

the office—insisting she take a break—surprising her on one occasion when she arrived back late from seeing a client and found him indulging in coffee and a lazy conversation with her secretary. He had the same bedazzling effect on Rachael as he had on every woman, Lee thought, amused, that day, hugging the secret satisfaction to herself that this man was hers.

Under his expert guidance, she learned the whereabouts of New York's lesser known art treasures, sharing his appreciation of them, enjoying discussing them with him, and, as June blossomed into full summer, she also found him a remarkable opponent for one of her other passions—tennis. He was good—very good, she discovered, although sometimes he would allow her to win. But, more often than not, that competitive, dominant streak of his forced him into showing his superb mastery of the game—and over her.

'You might sometimes take into account that I'm a woman!' she exclaimed good-humouredly, after losing yet another match to him one day after work. Towelling her damp skin, she watched him vault the net, looking as relaxed in his white shirt and shorts as if he hadn't yet begun the two punishing sets he'd taken her through in a sweltering eighty degrees. 'You could at least have the decency to look hot!'

'What's wrong, little Eve? Poor loser?' He tapped her lightly on the backside with the head of his racket before tossing it aside, the tantalising little action sending a tingle down Lee's spine. 'That's what comes of my letting you win too often,' he laughed. 'You can't take it when you lose.' His arm snaked around her middle, catching her hard against him, those thick, dark lashes lowering as his gaze caressed her tanned, lithe figure in the flattering sports dress. 'Don't you like surrendering to me?' His lips were just a hair's breadth from hers, his arm growing taut against the small of her back. She could feel the heat emanating from him, smell the rather evocative scent of his perspiration, and she gave a small, muted sound of acquiescence in her throat, body straining, on tiptoe, for the kiss he teasingly withheld.

He smiled lazily at her. 'Haven't you ever heard of hard-won rewards being the most enjoyable?' He was feathering kisses across the damp skin of her jaw, deliberately avoiding her lips in a heady arousal of her senses. 'Or even that you learn to appreciate things more if you're made to earn them, Coralie?'

Lee stiffened, wondering why he'd said that—for some reason suspecting that there was a subtle allusion to Richard Colyer's generosity to her in that whispered remark.

'What's that supposed to mean?' she queried cagily, drawing back a little, and, looking up into those strong, inscrutable features, had a sudden urge to tell him the truth. But a swift surge of pride stopped her. Why should she? she thought, hurting inside. 'Are you suggesting that things have always come too easily to me?' she challenged woundedly—certain of it—unable to stop herself adding, 'Like your father's money?'

Anger flitted across Jordan's face, lent a tautness to his jaw. 'That isn't what I meant—and you know it,' he said, in a low, controlled voice. 'And that's all in the past—so don't you ever throw that up in my face again.' He kissed her then, with a hard, punishing thoroughness that left her breathless and stirred that familiar, acute ache in her loins, before he held her away from him, giving her a slanted look. 'Why so touchy all of a sudden, Coralie?' he probed quietly—

gently—though there was a hard assessment in his eyes. 'Something worrying you?'

Pulling out of his grasp, she looked away, across the park where a dog was barking excitedly, where children were playing, their voices carried with the sweetness of new-mown grass on the humid, evening air. She was being touchy, and she knew it, even if she wasn't sure why. Perhaps it was the heat. Or more probably the strain she'd been under recently, trying to hang on to her magazine. There had been times, during the past few weeks, when she'd known the almost overwhelming urge to tell him about the difficulties she was facing—desperate for his advice. After all, that keen, enterprising brain hadn't made him a multi-millionaire without admirable insight and ingenuity, and she was sure he could have offered her some constructive recommendations for dealing with a floundering business. But she had made a promise to herself, a long time ago, that she'd never be dependent on any man— and she didn't think she could bear the humiliation of Jordan possibly deducing that she might be asking him—of all people—to bail her out. In fact, pride kept her from telling him a lot of things, the main one now that *Eve's Apple* had finally proved to be too much of a loss, and that, under pressure from the other directors, she was selling out. 'I'm thirsty,' she parried, picking up her racket without looking at him, so that he wouldn't see the tears of defeat glistening in her eyes. 'Let's get a drink.'

She heard him catch his breath—guessed that he was still angry with her for saying what she had—but, trudging away from him, she failed to see the dark, glittering emotion that was burning in his eyes, or the way those black brows knitted together, before he shrugged, scooped up his own racket and towel, and followed her off the court.

CHAPTER NINE

THE take-over went through smoothly enough. There had been two companies interested in the *Apple*, but the offer tendered by Carville Investments—a rapidly expanding publishing firm—had far exceeded the sum put forward by its rival, and it had been Carville's unexpected and irresistible offer, Lee realised, that had induced Peter, Clive and Marjorie to put pressure on her to sell. Though the new company's directors were pleasant enough, and their proposals didn't include axing any jobs, so that, at their request, Lee still retained her post as Editor-in-Chief, it was stupid, she knew, but she couldn't help feeling, as she stepped out of her office that first evening, that she had lost everything.

'Cheer up, pet.' Marjorie had been liaising with one of the reporters in the big open office that was the nerve centre of the journal, and she smiled understandingly when she saw Lee. 'This way, at least, we all get to keep our jobs, our mortgages and our sanity without any cut in salary,' she consoled, knowing exactly what was wrong. 'And I might just manage to save my marriage,' she appended drily. 'For the past few months, Don's been threatening divorce!'

She was only joking, Lee knew, although it didn't take much working out to realise that the company's problems would have put a strain on anyone's marriage, which was probably why Peter and Clive, too, had welcomed a take-over. At least now everyone could stop worrying, she thought, trying not to think of

151

herself as she made her way downstairs and out into the busy street.

'Hi! Like a lift?'

Vince was parked outside in his small green convertible, and Lee jumped at the offer, since her own car had been giving her problems again and was currently being repaired.

'What are you doing this evening, honey-bunch?' he queried when they were weaving their way through the heavy traffic, the towering skyscrapers looming down on them more stiflingly, Lee thought, than usual. 'Fancy a pizza?'

'Thanks, but I'm having a relaxing evening at home,' she sighed, looking forward to it after an extremely hectic day—longing to see Jordan, too, although, uneasily, she wondered if she would.

That evening in the park she'd made him angry, though she couldn't really understand why. But he'd made love to her that night with a fierceness she hadn't known in him before, taking her in an act of total mastery that had wrung a wild and uncontrolled response from her—had had her sobbing all that was in her heart out. But she hadn't seen him since, waking the following morning to an empty apartment and his short, rather impersonal note telling her he was going out of town. Though she told herself now that she was being silly, she couldn't help wondering if those abandoned moments, when she had so recklessly bared her soul to him, had started him thinking that she was getting too serious about him—if he didn't just want an uncomplicated affair.

'You're very involved with that guy, Colyer, aren't you?'

It was as if Vince had read her thoughts, and she

glanced up, startled. 'Am I?' she parried, wondering why he looked so serious.

'I'm fond of you, Lee,' he expressed then, blaring his horn at some driver who tried to cut in too close, 'and I don't want to see you get hurt. And getting too serious over a guy like that could be a recipe for disaster.'

She felt a sudden, unexpected gnawing feeling somewhere around her heart.

'I appreciate your concern,' she returned, a little acridly, not sure whether it was just because of what he had said or because his words had seemed to reinforce her own doubts of a moment ago. 'But I think I know Jordan a bit better than you do.'

'Do you?' He sent her a look that was almost reprimanding. 'And you're still besotted with the guy?'

'What do you mean?' she queried pointedly, an angry flush stealing across her cheeks. 'Just what are you getting at, Vince?'

He negotiated some traffic lights, pulling across a busy junction before replying. 'I know it's none of my business, Lee, and all right, Colyer gives all the outward appearance of forthrightness and integrity. Not to mention that he's been dished out with far more than his share of wealth, good looks and physical attraction this side of the Rockies, so I can understand why women virtually fall at his feet. Anyway, that's their problem, but you're my friend, and I think it's only fair to tell you that I don't like the things I've been hearing about him lately.'

An icy hand seemed to clutch at Lee's heart, and she shivered involuntarily in her thin blouse and skirt, though the sun was shining brilliantly above the imposing buildings.

'What *things*?' she asked indignantly, frowning, her

hair blowing wildly in the freedom of the open car. 'What exactly are you trying to tell me?'

He looked upset, she thought, swallowing—as if he wished he hadn't begun this line of conversation—and she knew him too well to know that he wouldn't deliberately hurt her, even if he was probably just a little bit jealous of the other man's glaring attributes.

'Tell me, Vince.'

He took a deep breath as he steered the convertible around a corner. 'It's just something I heard about his father—the way he treated him. It was at a party recently, from someone who was an old business associate or something of ol' man Colyer's. Apparently Jordan was in business with him originally, but because the ol' man wouldn't give him a whiphand, after some row or other Jordan pulled out. And then, to spite his father, he deliberately set up in the same line of business, in the same area, in direct opposition to him, with the result that ol' man Colyer eventually lost so much trade and custom to his son that he was forced to close that particular side of his business down. The man's got a lust for power, Lee.' His mouth pulled down one side. 'Particularly over women. But he'll tread on anyone who's in a weaker or more vulnerable position than he is. So perhaps you can understand my concern in seeing you getting involved with him. A guy like that will take everything you've got to give and leave you flat—that's how ruthless he is. He has to be—if he can do a thing like that to his own father.'

Well, he would be, Lee admitted reluctantly, if it were true. But she couldn't believe it was. There had been real pain in his eyes that day when he had told her about his relationship with Richard, although, contrarily, he hadn't actually explained the reason for the rift between them, she recalled unwillingly now.

He'd just said that there were differences of opinion. But it would take pretty drastic differences to drive a father to cutting a son out of his will. So was that the real reason behind Richard Colyer's action? That Jordan had deliberately forced him out of business?

The unwelcome thoughts chased around her brain, her heart heavy with doubt. But somehow she couldn't quite equate such extreme ruthlessness with the man she couldn't help but love. A man who showed such obvious care and concern for his uncle. Who sat children on his shoulder and talked to them like a friend. Surely, whoever had told Vince that story had got it all wrong? she mused, her earlier depression over losing *Eve's Apple* buried under the weight of what Vince had just told her.

She wouldn't accept it, though, and knew that she'd only have to ask Jordan if he called round tonight, to hear from his own lips that it wasn't true. She was desperate to see him, needing his assurance that nothing had changed between them since her foolish declaration of her love for him the other night; longing, too, for the comfort of his arms after the failure of her venture, and wondering, a little bit queasily, what he would say, as she didn't think he would be too pleased that she hadn't told him about it before. He didn't call that night, though—or the next—and she couldn't help feeling with a frightened, almost panicky feeling inside, that his lack of communication had an ominous ring of finality about it.

Working late the following evening, she was just locking her filing cabinet for the night when Rachael suddenly swept in with more than her usual sense of urgency.

'I've just heard some rather staggering news,' she

declared, her expression unusually perplexed. 'About Jordan Colyer.'

Lee's face went white. An accident! she thought, for no apparent reason, her breath locking in her lungs. 'About what?' Unwittingly, she backed against her desk for support, her mind suddenly tormented by the image of Jordan lying, injured, in a hospital somewhere, when she had known nothing about it.

'Well, Eddie just rang to say he'd be late picking me up,' Rachael explained, accounting for the reason she was still there. 'And he said that Carville Investments and Langman's—the firm he works for—are owned by the same holding company and that Jordan Colyer's recently taken over as kingpin. Which means that he owns *Eve's Apple*, doesn't it, you dark horse? You could have told us!' she exclaimed, obviously delighted to realise that the man was, in effect, now her lord and master.

Her first fears that something had happened to him now ebbing away, Rachael's revelation hit Lee like a blow below the belt.

Carville Investments was his? The *Apple* was his? But how could it be? she wondered with a sudden, numbing sense of betrayal. If he'd known she was in difficulties—selling out—he'd never have gone ahead and taken it over without offering to help her in some way first, would he? Not that she would have accepted any help from him, of course, but he would have offered, surely? she thought, trying to reason. He would never have done anything so underhanded as she was imagining.

Or would he?

Unbidden, what Vince had related to her about him earlier in the week loomed with abhorrent conviction in her brain.

If he could be as ruthless with his own father, then why not with her? True, there was no way she could have hung on to the *Apple* single-handed, but why hadn't he said something? Discussed it with her personally? Or didn't personal relationships come into it when he saw a business that was such easy-pickings as hers had been?

Pain stabbed her so that it was difficult to breathe, although—heaven only knew how—she managed to convey some light response to her secretary. But when the other woman had gone she sank down on to her chair, numerous bewildering questions suddenly flooding into her mind.

Had he, when he had asked her—on more than one occasion over the past few weeks—if anything was wrong, known all along? When he had imparadised her with his kisses, made her beg and sob with the pleasure of his lovemaking, had he been planning this. . .this take-over? A complete and outright possession of her magazine as unconscionably as he had taken possession of her heart and her body? But why? she wondered, in agonised perplexity. Why would he have wanted the *Apple*?

The anguished thoughts spun unanswered around her brain, and it wasn't until she heard the clock chime softly in the outer office that she realised how long she had been sitting there.

Numbly, she prepared to leave, making her way through the deserted larger office and into the corridor, then stopped, hearing a sound in the boardroom at the far end. She frowned, knowing that everyone, including the cleaners and the caretaker, had gone, and uncertainly she made her way towards it, noticing now the light coming through the gap where the door stood slightly ajar. She caught the murmur of voices and decided to investigate, gently pushing it a little wider, recognising two of the new directors, and the more authoritative, dark-suited figure, standing, poring over some papers on the table.

The small sob that escaped her brought Jordan's swift, upward glance her way. His whispered expletive said it all, and Lee looked at him with wounded, disbelieving eyes, feeling that at any moment she might possibly faint.

Instantly, though, Jordan was back in control. Tossing some instruction over his shoulder to the other two, he was hustling Lee away, back along the corridor to the privacy of her own office, snapping on the light.

'Why didn't you tell me?' she breathed numbly, her eyes only half registering how hot and weary he looked.

'I'm sorry.' He steeled himself with a deep breath, his chest expanding beneath the pure silk shirt. 'I didn't intend for you to find out this way.'

Lee stared at him, wondering how he could look so unperturbed—save for that slight flush across the well-sculpted cheekbones—while pain seemed to be eating her insides away.

'And just how was I supposed to find out?' she threw at him bitterly, a tremor in her voice. 'Were you going to break it to me gently? Or were you hoping I'd never get to find out that someone I. . .' loved, she nearly said, but instead murmured '. . .trusted. . .could go behind my back. . .do anything so low. . .?' She was near to tears, but she fought them back, sticking her chin out in defence against them.

She heard Jordan catch his breath, saw a muscle pull at the side of his mouth. 'I really do apologise, Coralie. I didn't realise your feelings for me were quite so magnanimous,' he delivered caustically, his words searing through her heart. With hurt, accusing eyes she saw him tug his tie loose, his movements jerky and impatient. 'You could have asked me for help if you'd wanted it, but no, you were too darn proud! You would have lost it anyway,' he stated categorically then, the cool, emotionless words falling like icicles on Lee's heart. He came and rested his hands lightly on the back of a chair beside the desk, hands which were long and well-tapered, hands which she was ashamed to find herself thinking, even now, could arouse and excite her. 'I would have thought you'd be thanking me, Coralie. It could have gone to a far less discerning purchaser than me. . .like the one you had lined up. . .who would probably have turned it into some cheap rag that wouldn't even have been worth reading, knowing the standard of their publications. As it is now——'

'*Thanking* you?' she exhaled with biting emphasis. 'For what? Stealing *Eve's Apple* from under my nose?'

'I didn't *steal* it,' he underlined with such a cool, restrained anger that Lee took a step back, afraid of his threatening mood. 'I paid very handsomely for that magazine, as you can darn well vouch! And it didn't appear to me to be too unreasonable to want to put my own money into it. After all. . .' He paused, almost as if he were hesitant to go on. Then, more quietly, 'It was Colyer money that financed it in the beginning, wasn't it?'

No, it damn well wasn't! Misery flowed like tar through her veins with the sudden dawning realisation. So that was it, she thought wretchedly. The money! Despite his claims that it was in the past, had he never really stopped resenting her for inheriting it? Had he seen her as only a symbol of his father's contempt for him every time he had looked at her—made love to her?

'You bastard,' she swore viciously, tortured by his actions, the doubts over what Vince had told her about him making her press woundedly on. 'You never could forgive me for being left that money, could you?' she uttered from a well of unbelievable anguish, and, with a crack in her voice, 'Is that why you've been amusing yourself with me for the past few weeks? Coming into the office? So you could get the feel of the place—take a look at the set-up before you finally took control of all I've ever worked for, everything that ever meant anything to me?' Because she remembered now that that day she'd come in and found him drinking coffee with Rachael, the woman had told her afterwards that he'd seemed so interested in how the journal functioned, she had actually shown him round, and Lee had imagined it was only a casual curiosity. How naïve she had been! 'What was it you wanted Jordan. . . compensation?' she finished on a small, hysterical little laugh.

Some dark emotion crossed his face and was swiftly obliterated, replaced by hard, indisputable anger. 'If you think that, Coralie, then you're more of a child than I ever imagined you to be,' he said hoarsely, turning away from her as though he didn't want to discuss it any more.

Stung by the almost insulting casualness of the dismissal, Lee moved over to grip the edge of her desk for support, wondering how he could act with such brutal detachment when her own heart felt as if it were bleeding.

'A child? Heaven's above! A saint would be mortally wounded!' The tortured exclamation ended on an incredulous little note. 'What a laugh you must have been having, taking me to bed with you, knowing how I felt about you. . .and all the time you were planning this——' She broke off, her tears threatening to reveal themselves, her hand going to her face to hide her weak and pointless emotion over him so that she didn't see the move he made towards her. Bitterly, she said, 'Well, congratulations, Jordan. Obviously, to you, personal relationships don't mean a thing! But I should have had more sense, shouldn't I, than to have expected you to mention it to me before you went ahead and bought me out? After all, I was only someone you were sleeping with——'

'What's that supposed to mean?' His hard demand cut across her unthinking words, the strong lines of his half-averted face taut and angry, his hands planted on his hips.

Lee swallowed, realising she had to say it now. 'Your father,' she uttered tremulously. 'I've heard you—you started up a business in direct opposition. . .'

Some inscrutable emotion darkened his eyes as he regarded her with a close, searching scrutiny. 'Who told you that?'

Lee hesitated, reluctant to inform him that it was something Vince had heard. 'Isn't it true?' she parried in a virulent tone, her blue-green eyes fixed accusingly on his, challenging him to deny it.

But he said, almost tonelessly, 'Yes, it's true,' an admission that made the blood drain out of Lee's cheeks, a cold, sick feeling invading her stomach. 'But if you want to listen to gossip, you'll invariably hear things that aren't too pleasant,' he stated, his mouth pulling grimly at the corners. 'And it seems to me I'm going to have to put some sense into that naïve little brain——'

'Stay away from me!' As he came towards her she moved around the desk, her hand closing around something cold and solid.

'Don't you dare!' Jordan's eyes flashed a hard, steely warning, but the paperweight had already left her hand, only the man's swift move to one side allowing it to miss its target and cannon into the soft pile of the carpet.

Pain lay like a lead weight in Lee's chest as she stared down at the gift he had given her, and she stifled a small sound as she saw the bitter irony of what it represented now. Her own dreams of paradise tossed brutally away with the knowledge of what he had done.

'I think I'd better come back when you can discuss this thing more rationally, Coralie.' There was a rough, raw quality to Jordan's voice. 'If I start losing my temper, it won't be with a paperweight, so for both our sakes I think I'd better leave now.'

She met the blaze of his eyes with the guarded injury of her own, but there was more in those strong lineaments, adding an almost desolate quality to their arresting structure. But then he was gone, the quiet closing of the door underlining that total self-possession and restraint in shaming contrast to the complete lack of her own.

She spent a sleepless night, tortured not only by the knowledge that Vince had been right about Jordan, but that he could have treated her so indiscriminately, too. How he must have resented her, she thought, a small sob escaping her in the lonely darkness of her room, so that when she got up the following morning her eyes were red, her face looked drawn and pale, and she felt like death.

Still, life had to go on, she told her reflection silently in the bathroom mirror, without really believing it. She would much rather have crawled back under the duvet and stayed there!

Carefully, though, she attempted to disguise the

glaring evidence of how she was feeling with a few cosmetic touches, even putting on her newest outfit to try and pretend to the world that she wasn't going to pieces inside. And it worked!

'Holy smoke!' was Vince's startled comment when he saw her. He came around her desk, making a leisurely study of the upswept hair, the deep pink of lips and nails that matched the cerise of her blouse—a vivid contrast to the beautifully tailored black suit— and he whistled softly at the provocative side-split of a skirt that offered an alluring glimpse of slender leg. 'Who's this for?' he asked.

There isn't anyone, Lee nearly said, but stopped herself in time. That would pose too many awkward questions which she didn't feel like answering at that moment. Such as that it was over between her and Jordan. He hadn't as much as telephoned this morning. Not that she wanted to hear from him, she assured herself unconvincingly. But she would have thought, in the circumstances, at the very least he would have rung, although she wasn't really sure what she expected him to say. That none of it was true? And that was like wishing for the moon, she thought self-beratingly, hurting unbearably inside.

But she merely offered Vince a wan smile, so that he sensed her melancholy, but misinterpreted the reason for it, saying gently, 'Going down with the flag flying?'

He sounded sympathetic and Lee warmed towards him, glad at that moment of his friendship. He understood better than anyone what the magazine had meant to her.

'No, Vince,' she uttered, and her eyes held a sudden glimmer of that purposefulness he knew so well. 'I'm not totally sunk yet.'

She could see his curiosity was aroused, although she

didn't enlarge. But during the sleepless hours last night, she had come to a decision. Jordan Colyer might have taken everything from her love to her self-respect, but if he thought she would simply lie down and let him take her magazine, too—well, was he in for a shock! And she'd let him have it. Now. Today. And in the only way she could!

She had a queasy feeling in her stomach, though, as she rang his office a little later, and her heart lurched when she was put through to his extension, although it was Madeline who answered.

'He's not here,' was the clipped response when Lee asked to speak to Jordan, and the woman sounded surprised, Lee thought, to be hearing from her. She hadn't spoken to Madeline since that awful night on Alec's patio, and she wondered if Jordan's secretary even knew that Jordan had been seeing her. 'He's in Bermuda,' Madeline went on casually.

For a moment, Lee was too stunned to speak. How could he do what he had done and then fly to Bermuda as if nothing had happened? The calculating, heartless. . .Tears mingled with anger, and her fingers played agitatedly with the telephone wire as she steadied her voice enough to ask, 'When will he be back?'

'I really don't know.' Madeline might not have been being deliberately unhelpful, but Lee was struck by the awful thought suddenly that, if she was, then perhaps she had been instructed to—that perhaps now that Jordan had taken everything he wanted from her, he was using his secretary to give her the brush-off like some objectionable business associate he didn't want to see. Well, he was in for a surprise! 'Was it anything important?' she heard Madeline ask.

Lee braced herself, hoping she could sound nonchalant. 'Yes, it's about the take-over.'

'What take-over?'

Madeline didn't know? Surprised, Lee breathed a silent sigh of relief. So Jordan had at least spared her that much, she thought, wondering why she should feel at all grateful to him for that consideration. But she did. And guessed that perhaps he'd felt this thing was solely between him and her.

'I need to speak to Jordan personally,' she asserted, a little more confidently now. 'Will he be back on Monday?'

'I shouldn't think it very likely.' Madeline sounded vaguely curious, but somehow less condescending than usual, Lee thought, as the woman offered, 'I could give him a message if he rings in before five o'clock if you like, although after that my duties as his secretary end. If you decide to speak to someone else, then from Monday you'll have to go through the new girl,' she informed Lee, adding, with a pure pride she obviously couldn't conceal, 'In just over a week from now, I'm going to be on my honeymoon.'

So that explained her more congenial mood today, Lee thought. The prospect of marriage.

Telling her there was no message, she rang off, wondering why Jordan hadn't told her his secretary was leaving. But there were a lot of things he'd omitted to mention recently, she reminded herself bitterly. Like his acquisition of the magazine. The real reason for the rift between him and his father. And now, knowing how much he had hurt her, leaving New York without a word. Oh, dear lord! How could he?

Brushing impatiently at the tears she couldn't control, she rammed the drawer of her desk closed with unusual vehemence and buzzed through to Rachael next door.

'I'm going home,' was all she said to her surprised

secretary. She had to. She simply couldn't sit in the office any longer, just waiting for Jordan to call. She felt she would crack up if she did. 'I'll be back in a day or two.'

'What happens if something crops up that only you can deal with?' Rachael sounded flabbergasted, probably unable to understand why her boss suddenly seemed to be going under after her hard-fought, if vain, attempts to keep the *Apple*. It wasn't like her. 'Is it all right if I contact you at the apartment?'

'No,' was Lee's very decisive response. 'I'll be in Bermuda.'

CHAPTER TEN

ALEC was propped up on the couch in his study, a tartan rug over his legs, and the autocratic face broke into a smile when the Bermudian showed Lee in.

'Come here, my dear. Let me look at you.' The hands that took hers were warm and mottled and strong, and his keen regard too wise to her pallor beneath the cleverly applied make-up, and the tear-stung eyes that even dark shadow and several layers of mascara couldn't hide. 'What's wrong?' he asked gently.

Lee swallowed, weak from the effort of trying not to succumb to an overwhelming urge to pour out her feelings to a fatherly ear.

'Nothing,' she lied, determined not to worry him with it. It was her problem, after all. 'But what about you?' He looked well, but a little tired, she thought, and then noticed the dark bruising along his left wrist. 'What have you done to yourself?' she asked, her forehead creasing worriedly.

'Oh! Everyone makes too much fuss,' he complained, with a weary smile, waving Lee's concern aside. 'Even a baby falls down when it's trying to walk. I can get about all right with sticks now, although the stairs got the better of me early this morning, and I'm afraid Matthew decided I'd broken every bone in my body and felt he ought to get Jordan out here. Worried him sick, of course, and he flew out straight away.' Which he would, Lee automatically acknowledged silently, without knowing why. Somehow she couldn't

equate this caring side of him with the ruthlessness with
which he had treated his father—her. 'A bit too
adventurous again.' The man winked at her with self-
chastening mockery. 'Did he send for you?' he was
suddenly querying.

Lee shook her head, baffled. Why would he think
that? 'I needed to see him about something important.'
She looked questioningly towards the door. 'Is he
around?'

Already her stomach muscles were tightening from
the mere thought of seeing Jordan, because this time
would be the last. After she had done what she had
come here to do, there wouldn't be any need for her to
see him ever again. But the very concept of a future in
which he shared no part sent needles of anguish
through her, and over her misery she heard Alec say
lightly, unaware, 'It must be important for you to come
all this way to see him.' He was studying her intently,
and he seemed to pick his words carefully as he said,
'You know he's decided to get married, don't you?'

It was like being hit with a tangible object. Suddenly
she didn't know how much more she could take. But
she had been as naïve as Jordan had accused her of
being, she realised, with a heart-crushing debilitation,
as all at once things became clear. How could she have
imagined, when Madeline had mentioned her honeymoon, that the woman would be marrying anyone else
but her boss? Madeline had been besotted with him,
Lee remembered torturedly, and they had known each
other for a long time. But why had he nurtured her
feelings for him—made her want him, she agonised, if
in the end he had intended to settle down with
Madeline? Had she bruised his pride that much in
proving him wrong about her when she had surren-
dered to him here, back in the spring? Or did he really

resent her that much? Realised how vulnerable her feelings were and planned this. . .this humiliation? she thought, tears blinding her.

Averting her eyes so that the man wouldn't see, Lee took a deep breath, summoning all her courage to say, 'Well, it's about time, isn't it?' She even managed a little laugh, but its tremor gave a lie to her careless response, and she felt Alec's eyes on her, not twinkling today, but sombre with some other emotion. Pity? She stifled a sob. She didn't think she could bear it!

'You know, Lee. . .I rather hoped that you and he. . .Still. . .' A movement of his hands seemed to underline the finality of the situation—the futility in Lee's heart. 'If you want to see him urgently, you'll have to go down to the cottage. When he realised I wasn't on the way out, he took off to attend to one or two things that needed doing down there. I think he wants to get the place up to scratch for the honeymoon, so he's likely to be there for a few hours yet. Ask Matthew to drive you. Or you can take the car yourself if you like.'

Keeping her emotions on a tight rein, Lee thanked him and plumped for the latter, glad to get out of the house. Like his nephew, Alec was too shrewd, and it wouldn't have taken much for her to have broken down under that pitying sagacity, she thought torturedly, manoeuvring the heavy car along the Bermuda lanes. Everywhere was a blaze of colour—bougainvillaea, hibiscus and other flamboyant shrubs she couldn't name adding purple and red flames to the gardens and hedgerows, while a mixture of sweet scents drifted in through the car window on the warm breeze. Summer was wearing on, though, golden-brown berries replacing the fragrant flower clusters of the Pride of India, Lee noticed as she pulled up outside the cottage, tension gripping her insides when she saw the long, low sports car Jordan kept on the island, standing there gleaming beneath it.

He answered her knock almost immediately, casually dressed in blue denim from head to foot, his gaping shirt exposing his tanned, masculine chest.

'Coralie!' He looked as surprised as she had expected him to, surprised and a little bit shocked, too, she thought, although he said remarkably calmly, 'Won't you come in?'

She responded to his courteous gesture by brushing past him with her chin in the air, trying not to acknowledge how that subtle male scent of him with that glaring virility of his could still affect her, in spite of everything.

The place smelt strongly of paint. There were dust-sheets on the floor, and in the doorway between the lounge and the kitchen was an open pot of white undercoat with a brush lying across it, and some metal steps, too, folded against the wall.

'Decorating?' she queried icily, numb inside.

A dark eyebrow lifted at the obvious chill in her voice, but he merely stooped to pick up the paintbrush, and said, 'That's right. And I'd better carry on with this door, if you don't mind, otherwise it'll be too tacky to finish. Now, what brings you here?' he queried, dropping to his haunches to work on the lower half. 'Obviously, from the sound of things, not the pleasure of my company,' he remarked with a dry cynicism that made Lee want to lash out at him.

One glance round showed her things that were too painfully familiar: the paintings, the fireplace, the settee. . .She shut her mind against the unwelcome memory of that first time, and uttered with as little emotion as possible, 'Alec tells me you're getting married.' Let him think she didn't care! 'Is that right?'

He paused from his brushwork and glanced up into her eyes, his so dark and reflective that she felt that old, cruel response rise unbidden in her blood. She saw his chest muscles flex before he stated, clearly put out. 'Tact never was Alec's strongest virtue.' And with that gaze still holding hers, as though he dared her to object, he said simply, 'Well?'

Well, what? What was he expecting? Her congratulations? Pain lacerated her with claws of steel, and she swallowed, feeling an uncomfortable dryness in her throat.

'Does she know?' she queried shakily, wondering how he could carry on painting so calmly while she felt she had barely the strength to stand.

He looked up at her again, a line between his eyes. 'Does she know what?' he enquired, pointedly. As if he didn't have a clue!

Tension made her throat constrict, her insides clench sickeningly. 'Does he know that. . .that up until a few days ago you. . .' She was floundering, tormented by the bitter-sweet memory of how it felt making love with him, and he wasn't helping her at all, calmly placing his brush in a jar of spirit and standing up, wiping his hands on the rag. 'Does she know that you've been taking me to bed with you?' she got out at last, a sob in her voice.

He looked at her from under his lashes, his lips curling in a travesty of a smile. 'Yes, she does,' he said laconically, moving into the kitchen to toss the rag on to the steel drainer.

Lee followed him, pulling her jacket closely around her, careful to avoid the freshly painted door. Her eyes were incredulous as she stared after Jordan's broad back. 'You mean. . .you told her?' She couldn't believe he could do such a thing. 'And she. . .she doesn't *care*?'

He turned round, leaning against the sink, his gaze running over her gentle curves beneath the stylish black suit, his lips—still bearing that hurtfully mocking smile—compressing, as though he, too, were remembering the passionate nights they had shared—the secret pathways of her body.

'Why should she?' he remarked, his hand coming to rest on the tapering narrowness of his waist, the movement tugging at his shirt, exposing more of that hard, hair-sprinkled chest. 'She was perfectly aware of what was happening. Or at least, I believe she was,' he appended wryly.

She couldn't understand how he could be amusing himself with her like this, suddenly very close to losing control. 'My goodness!' she exclaimed, not caring if he did see now how deeply she was hurting inside. 'I always thought Madeline was thick-skinned, but compared with you she's made of spider's silk!' Colour stole across her cheeks, unusually pale against the dark elegance of her upswept hair. She felt like collapsing in tears, but she had to hang on to her self-possession for her pride's sake—and for the one reason she had come back to Bermuda today. Her chin lifted, exposing the smooth column of her throat above the vivid cerise blouse, and very calmly she said, 'What you do with your private life doesn't concern me in the slightest.' If only that were true! 'And I might have been blinded enough to let you take everything I had to give, but you're not taking *Eve's Apple*. I want it back, Jordan. . .and I intend to get it with the only means available to me.'

Surprise crossed his face at her purposeful little speech, his gaze tugging down over her in such a deliberate and disconcerting appraisal of her body that Lee brought her tongue nervously to her top lip, then saw the slow smile that gesture induced.

'What are you going to do, sweetheart?' he asked quietly, sickeningly amused, yet she sensed anger in him, too. 'Seduce me for it?'

Her colour deepened with the agony inside her. How could he make a joke of it—treat her with so little feeling—when he knew how much she cared about him? she thought, sick with pain—with misery.

'That's just about all I could expect from you!' she threw at him angrily, her hands shaking as she rummaged for something in her handbag. Finding the small piece of paper, she flung it down on the drainer, the movement causing her arm to accidentally brush his so that she recoiled from him as if he carried a thousand-volt charge. 'It's your father's money, Jordan—every single cent he left me—intact! But I'm afraid it doesn't come with interest accrued, because that's been going towards research into rare blood diseases for the past eight years!' A thing from which Richard had died. But she had vowed, from the day she had inherited the money, that she would use it to help others who might be suffering in the same way—that she would never spend a cent of it on herself. Had it been anyone other than Jordan in this take-over, she knew she wouldn't even have considered using it now, because buying him out and having *Eve's Apple* under her own control again meant having to sell her apartment—move into something smaller and cheaper—because she was going to need all the capital she could lay her hands on if she wasn't going to let down everyone who would be depending on her. But at least, this way, she could salve some of her pride, hang on to all she had worked for, and at the same time give Jordan the money which, as far as she was concerned, should always have been his. 'I never once regarded it as mine—despite all your false assumptions about me,' she informed him grievously, blue eyes misty from her tumultuous emotions. 'Well, now it's yours, and since you've managed to humiliate me in every way you set out to, perhaps you're satisfied at last. So just go ahead and make the necessary arrangements for the *Apple*'s transfer to me, and then there'll never be any need for us to see each other again.'

The choking sob in her voice would have betrayed her if she hadn't finished then, and almost blindly her eyes registered the mixture of emotions on Jordan's face, ranging from shock to something she imagined looked remarkably like pain. But then his expression hardened, a steely anger replacing everything else and, with hands clenched at his sides, he said scathingly, 'And supposing it isn't enough?'

'Not enough?' Lee stared at him, appalled, baffled by the rough quality of his voice. 'Good gracious! That's nearly triple. . .'

'My dear girl,' he drawled, in a tone thick with reproach, 'contrary to your unflattering opinions of me, everything in my world isn't esteemed solely for its monetary value. I'll admit it has its uses, but I'm afraid this isn't one of them,' and to her stark amazement he picked up the cheque and began tearing it up, letting the pieces drop carelessly to the floor. 'I'd prefer something a little more complimentary—like trust. . .' his mouth tightened grimly '. . .if you've any inkling of what the word means. And, crazy though I might be at this precise moment, Coralie—*you*.'

She failed to digest what he was saying about trust, too astounded by that last, blatant admission. She took a step back, clutching her small bag to her with fingers that registered the hard thudding in her breast. 'You're not for real,' she accused, breathlessly—flabber-gasted—her eyes sparking an angry warning. 'Do you really think I'd still want you after——'

'Yes.' His indisputable certainty made her pulses throb, her throat constrict. 'You might have me labelled as a big bad heel, but you wanted me even when you thought I hated you, and we both know I'd only have to touch you now to turn you into a wild, abandoned little wanton just begging me to make love to her.'

'That's not true!' she flung at him, fear prickling along her spine.

'No?' He was moving towards her, his eyes angry and hard, his face so determined that she started to back away.

'After what you did to your father? What you've done to me? You're callous and conceited and——'

'For heaven's sake, watch the paint!'

She missed kicking the pot by a fraction of an inch, shooting out a hand to steady herself, which she quickly retracted with a pained grimace when she realised that the door-jamb was wet. But Jordan was still coming, and with such a feral gleam in his dark eyes that she let out a panicky, 'Don't you touch me!'

She had always thought that one day her temper would make her do something she would regret. Or perhaps it was just fear—the dread that any second he was going to prove himself right—because, shamefully, she still wanted him! She only knew that one moment she had a near-full pot of white undercoat in her hand, and that the next it was empty, Jordan's futile shout awakening her to the fact that she had just hurled the entire contents straight at him.

Horrified, she watched him drag his hands down the

front of his now predominantly white shirt, wiping away the surplus, though there were splashes all over his jeans, too, and on the quarry-tiled floor behind him.

'I—I'm sorry. I didn't mean. . .'

One look at his face and she was changing her mind about saying anything. She'd gone too far this time, she realised, seeing the grim cast of his features.

'OK, sweetheart, you've asked for it.'

'No!' Seeing the determination in him, Lee made to flee, but was too late, and felt the grip of hard, slippery fingers around her wrist. 'No, please! I didn't mean. . .No, let me go! You're covered. . .'

'Aren't I just?' A hard satisfaction gave a humourless curl to his mouth. 'And you're going to share the pure enjoyment of it with me, darling.'

'No!'

His hands seemed to be everywhere at once—on her exposed skin in the V of her blouse, running possessively across her breasts, and down, down over the beautiful black suit, leaving a visible white brand of possession wherever they touched. She was fighting him for all she was worth, using hands, feet and teeth, but he merely laughed deep in his throat and pulled her against him.

She gave a small gasp of protest as the wet warmth of him penetrated her blouse, as he began rubbing his paint-splashed body hard and deliberately against hers.

'No! Let me go!' Panic filled her as his intimate action gave rise to that traitorous soaring in her blood, a self-disgust that had her trying to jerk away from him, and with such force that she fell back against the steps, sending them crashing noisily to the floor, losing her balance in the process, with the result that they both ended up on the dust-sheeted carpet.

'Are you all right?'

Jordan's solicitude seemed misplaced after everything else he had done, but Lee couldn't answer,
battling against the sensations that were tingling
through her from the sheer weight of him on top of
her.

'Let me go!' Those hard shoulders resisted the
pummelling of her fists with mocking invincibility, and,
drowning in her own misery, suddenly, shamefully, she
was sobbing, her hands dropping away from him in
hopeless defeat.

'For heaven's sake, Coralie—come to your senses!
Do you really think I *wanted* to hurt you—in any way
at all?'

His words, raw with emotion, had her looking at him
with wet, bewildered eyes. His skin appeared drawn
across those well-defined bones, and there was an
almost pained groove between his eyes.

'I didn't take *Eve's Apple* away from you—well,
perhaps temporarily—but it was so that I could give it
back to you,' he confused her even more by saying,
placing his hands over hers at shoulder-level—hands
that were warm and strong and unbelievably sticky. 'I
wanted to do something—anything—to try and make
up for the way I'd treated you in the past, and when I
found out about the financial problems you were
having, it provided me with the means of at least
making a start. I knew how much the magazine meant
to you, and I couldn't bear to see you lose it to that
cheap rag merchant you were intending to sell out to,
but I didn't intend at first to take it over quite as I did.
I would much rather you'd confided in me—talked to
me about it, so that we could have sorted things out
together. It made me angry when you didn't, but I'd
already realised that you'd probably die first rather
than ever come to me—or any man—for help. Why,

Coralie?' His eyes probed hers, almost wounded in their intensity. 'Because taking a man's money would have made you feel too much like your mother?' He answered her startled murmur—the hard question in her eyes—with a slight inclination of his head. 'Oh, yes, I know about that. One lunchtime when I called round to see you and you weren't there, I bumped into Vince and he was very quick to put me in the picture.'

'He had no right!' Her forehead creasing, Lee wriggled under him in an attempt to free herself, though his response was to apply a slight pressure of his body to keep her still.

'He had every right,' he riposted, 'in so far as it helped me to understand you a little bit better, although I don't think your photographer friend really intended doing me any favours. I think, in a way, he was trying to warn me off, because he told me how sensitive and vulnerable you were—which I already knew—but that I didn't stand a chance with you because you'd never settle for a man who would make you feel dependent upon him financially—all of which made me suspect that he's half in love with you himself,' he interjected with a grimace. 'But he told me then about your mother. She left solely for the lure of another man's money, didn't she, Coralie?'

She could only nod in response, filled with the hurt and shame she had always felt because of her mother's behaviour—her own frank admission that she was leaving her husband for the luxury he could never provide.

'When I accused you of being a gold-digger—only after my father's money—I didn't realise then just what I was doing to you. I didn't realise then how deep the wounds were. I didn't know anything about you. All I knew was I wanted to hurt you for hurting my father—as I thought—perhaps even for having his affection when I didn't,' he was adding with a self-deprecating grimace, 'not realising that in doing so I was labelling you the same as your mother. And then, back in the spring, when you came to Bermuda. . .' There was a hoarse quality to his voice. 'For goodness' sake! Can't you understand how I had to try to make it up to you somehow—why I did what I did?'

That unmistakable sincerity in his voice shocked her into speechlessness, the realisation of his motive leaving her numb—confused. How could he pretend to have cared for his father when, contrarily, he'd admitted to being as ruthless as he had? And making himself her lover—had that been just another move in his plans to make amends—to be kind to her? she wondered crushingly—bitterly—tears burning her eyes. Or had he merely accepted the delights of her body as a bonus? A little extra thrown in while he'd purged himself of his past injustice towards her, before he left with a clear conscience to marry Madeline?

A sob broke from her lips. She couldn't bear it!

She struggled against him—against the sensations stirring in her from the long, hard length of him across her, which was melding into her softness with a sticky fusion of white paint.

'Let me go!'

He didn't, only rolling to one side when she winced beneath his weight, though an arm across her midriff still restrained her.

'I tried to get you to talk to me—more than once—but you wouldn't,' he continued, 'and I knew that if I'd told you I wanted to help you, you would have refused. Just like your father refused mine when he tried to help *him*,' he said, almost censuringly then. 'Well, you're certainly *his* daughter, Coralie—not your mother's—just as proud and just as stubborn——'

'Don't say things like that about my father!' She sat up quickly, instantly defensive. She felt wretched, and undignified, too, covered in white paint. 'He was kind and unselfish and always thought of everyone before himself, so how can you say that? You didn't even know him. Did you?' she enquired suddenly, head tilted, baffled as to what he meant about his father trying to help hers—as to how he knew.

Jordan raised himself up, his dark eyes level with hers. 'No, I didn't know him,' he acceded, quietly.

'So what makes you so qualified to make judgements about him?' she said woundedly. 'And how did you know what happened between your father and mine? You weren't on speaking terms with Richard, were you?' And not that it mattered—not that anything mattered any more, she thought torturously—but she held her breath and, in a lowered tone, pressed, 'Did—did you really set up in business against him?'

The deep chest expanded, paint matting the wiry hairs that curled over his shirt.

'Yes,' he said heavily, 'but not at all for the reasons you've probably been thinking.' He paused, then went on, 'It was in the original company back in Newfoundland. Every subsidiary and division of the Colyer Group—pulp, paper, packaging—had been born out of that timber business that my grandfather had started. It was still flourishing when my father took it over. But then competition got tough and we were hit badly. I knew we had to find new methods if we were to keep the Newfoundland business alive, but my father was very old-fashioned in his thinking, and hated change. His way was right—or so he believed—and he wouldn't adapt, or listen to any suggestions I tried to make. We started losing money, but he wouldn't let me put any of my own ideas into action. Colyers looked like being squeezed out of Newfoundland altogether, and I just couldn't stay there and watch our first company—something my grandfather had striven for all his life—just fold up. So I pulled out and started up on my own. My sole aim was to try to retrieve the trade we'd lost to our competitors—keep the Colyer name the force it had always been in Newfoundland—and I succeeded to the point that I began to hope my father would see that my innovations had paid off—that he'd join forces with me, so that together we'd have a far stronger and more viable company than we'd ever had before, but. . .' He gave a gesture of utter frustration and futility. 'He closed down and moved away to manage one of his New York companies instead. I don't know why. Pride, maybe, because he didn't want to admit he'd been wrong. As I said before. . .' his mouth pulled in self-deprecation. '. . .it's a family trait. Or maybe. . .maybe he knew then that he was ill and didn't have the will—or the energy—to want to start fighting back. . .' The broad chest lifted on a deep sigh. 'Anyway, I thought he died thinking the worst. But I've been wrong about so many things, Coralie. About you. About him. Believing all these years that he used you to hurt me—emotionally, if not in a material way, because the money never mattered,' and with deprecation in his eyes—his voice, 'even if you wanted to think it did. But, after all this time, today I finally found out the truth.'

Lee lifted her gaze to his, a puzzling question in the dark desolation of her eyes. 'What do you mean?' she whispered, wanting to get away from him, though curiosity—the self-castigation in Jordan's voice—was compelling her to stay.

'I presume my father told you how my mother died?'

She nodded, wondering what that had to do with anything.

'Did he ever mention to you that I was with her in that fire?'

Shocked, Lee shook her head. 'No.'

'It was in a hotel in New York. My father was combining pleasure with a business trip, and so wasn't there with us that night. There was some electrical fault, so they said—the whole suite was ablaze even before the Fire Department arrived, and my mother didn't have a chance. I wouldn't have made it either, but for a young man who was working his way around the States and who happened to be in the hotel that night. He heard a baby crying and somehow managed to get in, although no one seemed to think he would get out alive. But he did, and he brought me with him. A man I always knew I owed my life to, but whom I never had the chance to meet. Your father, Coralie.'

Incredulously, she stared at him, unable to take it in. 'But how? I mean. . .how do you know. . .?'

'My father told Alec that he'd met the man again just a few months before he died. Apparently, just after the fire, my father wanted to reward yours in the only way he knew—financially—but your father refused to accept any form of payment. He said he was only doing what anyone would have done, and that he didn't want anyone making a hero out of him—modest as he was—which is probably why you never got to hear about it. However, when my father discovered, years later, that yours was not only living in New York, but was in financial difficulties, he tried to help him then, but the man still wouldn't accept a thing. The only thing he asked was that if anything happened to him, for a while, until you were old enough, my father took care of you. My father didn't actually tell Alec that he was ill himself, only that when he died, as I was financially sound, he'd leave his money to the daughter of the man he felt indebted to.' Briefly, he hesitated, and then, 'He made Alec swear never to tell me. . .that if I ever found out. . .I'd think him a weak old fool.' The tremor in that deep voice betrayed the depth of his feeling for the father he'd thought had died despising him, and, from the way he turned away from her, she knew that all that emotion would be there, in his eyes. Hers were swimming with tears, too; because of her father's bravery, because of Richard's real motives when she had thought them so cruel, but mainly because she knew now why she'd always felt so drawn to Jordan. Some people might have called it Fate—he was her soul-mate, and she'd been created by the man who had saved his life, solely to love him. And if Fate were kind, he would have loved her in return. But it wasn't. And he was marrying someone else.

'Why did Alec suddenly decide to tell you now?' she asked with a trembling, heart-torn bitterness, because he'd left it just a little bit too late, she thought, although she understood now why he'd remained so hospitable towards her when Madeline had exposed her that night.

'He knew I was seeing you, and probably guessed from my mood when I got here this morning that things weren't right between us,' Jordan elucidated. 'I guess he probably thought I still needed convincing that I was wrong about you.' And more softly, 'Little knowing what a hard lesson I learned in being made to realise it for myself.'

Yes, in her reckless and so willing surrender to him, she thought torturedly, pain ripping across her heart.

Quickly she got to her feet.

'Where are you going?' Strong, tacky fingers were around her wrist as he brought himself upright, stopping her in her tracks.

'I—I've got to clean up,' she quavered, knowing that if she didn't leave soon she would break down completely, and she couldn't bear the humiliation of that. Trying to tug away from his relentless hold, a lump in her throat threatening to choke her, she was begging, '*Please*.'

A muscle twitched in the strong jaw. 'I want you to stay.'

The statement hung on the air, silencing and heavy between them, twisting like a knife in Lee's heart. Why was he doing this to her? she wondered torturedly. Couldn't he see he was tearing her apart?

'I can't,' she protested, still trying to pull free, but his grip tightened inexorably.

'Don't you love me?'

She met his eyes with a tormented look in her own. 'Isn't that rather an unfair question in the circumstances?' she uttered bitterly, brows knitting in anguish.

'Why?' he urged. As if he didn't know!

'Because you're getting married!' she flung at him, her tears suddenly having their own way and welling into her eyes.

Through blurred vision she saw that hard mouth quirk. And very softly he said, 'Well, not exactly. She hasn't entirely agreed to it yet. But do I take it from those tears, little Eve, that you'd be unhappy at the thought of me marrying anyone else.' His fingers trailed along her cheek, melting her resistance to him, their astringent smell tingling in her nostrils. 'You do love me, don't you?'

His eyes refused to release hers, and, trying as she

was to make sense of what he had just said, all she could do now was murmur truthfully, 'Yes.'

'Then why don't you accept my proposal?' His gaze was dark and intense and very sincere, and Lee's pulses were suddenly leaping out of control.

'But I thought. . .'

'You thought what?' he prompted half-chidingly.

'I thought. . .that you and Madeline. . .'

'*Madeline?*' He emphasised the name as if nothing could ever be more unlikely. 'Well, I know you'd dreamed up some hypothetical woman in your imagination, sweetheart, but I didn't imagine for one moment it would be. . .' He gave a low laugh as though the thought amused him. 'My relationship with Madeline has never been anything more than a casual flirtation. We've never even been lovers, if that's what you've been imagining.'

'But she said. . .' she had to think back to remember exactly what Madeline Eastman had told her. '. . .that she'd be on her honeymoon,' she related, puzzled. 'And Alec. . .he said you were getting married. . .'

Jordan's mouth pulled wryly. 'Probably testing your reaction to see if he could aid the course of true love, meddling old devil that he is. And yes, Madeline will be on her honeymoon next week, but not with me. She's had a whirlwind affair with some high-ranking naval administrator, and gave notice less than two weeks ago.'

'Why didn't you tell me?' she queried softly, a deep, soul-lifting warmth spreading through her, replacing the misery that had racked her when she'd arrived.

Jordan expelled an almost impatient sigh. 'My dearest, I've had enough to contend with, with the take-over and wondering how I could possibly get you to trust me enough to explain why I did it, so that I'm afraid my secretary's arrangements were the last thing on my mind.' He took her chin between his thumb and forefinger, placing a small smudge of paint there, too. 'I love you, Coralie. And, crazy though it seems, I think I always have. Even when my father died and you were leaving that house, you looked at me with those big hungry eyes—so young, so vulnerable—and, as much as I wanted to hurt you, I wanted to put my arms around you, too—comfort you—and the feeling made me even angrier with you. I thought you were some sort of witch who'd woven a spell over my father and was trying the same with me. It seemed indecent to be so affected by someone I thought I hated. So drawn. . .'

So he had felt it, too, she realised, her heart swelling—that subconscious recognition of a true mate that had been there almost from the beginning.

'I know I'm rich, and I do apologise for that,' he said drily then. 'And I like a woman who's independent, too, but not if it's at the expense of love. . .of trust. . .' His eyes were suddenly almost appealing to hers. 'Will you have me?' he whispered, brushing the small scar on her temple with lips that were tender and warm. 'Accept the *Apple* as a wedding present, as I intended it to be? Something we can build again together—watch grow strong and healthy.' He gave a little chuckle. 'Like our children?' And in a voice that trembled with emotion, 'Like our love?'

Tears sprang to her eyes again, but this time tears of unsurmountable joy in realising the feeling this man had for her—and only her—the sensitivity behind the invincible strength.

'I've got a terrible temper,' she reminded him, by way of acceptance. 'Do you think you can cope with that?'

He gave her a twisted smile. 'I'll just have to remember to duck now and then, won't I?' he acceded, pulling her towards him, adding with a low, and more playful, chuckle, 'But just think of the fun I'll have working out new and delightful ways for you to make recompense to me!'

'What do you mean?' she demanded, pulling back from him in mock indignation, a little tingle of excitement bringing a flush stealing across her cheeks.

He laughed, his arm tightening against her spine, the muscular strength of his aroused body sending a sharp thrill arrowing through hers. 'Simply that there's a penalty for covering me in paint, little one,' he murmured, half-hooded eyes smiling down on her comparatively slight stature. 'And it starts in the shower.'

He was still laughing, but he meant it, she realised deliciously, body tingling from the excitingly sensual threat his voice had held.

'Promise?' she murmured with a tantalising little smile, moving provocatively against his hard, lean warmth.

But for answer he was crushing her to him, the hungry acknowledgement of his mouth on hers assuring her of much more than any words ever could. Then he was lifting her up, up into a world of laughter and sunlight, and such a sweet golden lethargy of desire— although, before she allowed it to engulf her completely, silently she offered up a little prayer of gratitude to her father for giving her this man.

It was much later, nestling against the warm velvet of Jordan's shoulder, that she heard him whisper softly, 'Happy, little Eve?'

How could she be anything else? she wondered dreamily, in amazement, remembering his passion—

his infinite tenderness. She had her man, and she still had the *Apple*, too.

Snuggling into him, she murmured her soft acquiescence, lashes half parting to the evening sunlight playing through the leaves of the tall tree outside. A breeze lifted its higher branches, sending shadows of caressing fingers across the duvet and their interlocked limbs. And, in that inspired moment, its various names chased, like mischievous children, across the fringes of her consciousness. A Pride of India. A Persian Lilac. A Paradise Tree. . .

HARLEQUIN *Temptation*

Give in to Temptation! Harlequin Temptation

The story of a woman who knows her own mind, her own heart . . . and of the man who touches her, body and soul.

Intimate, sexy stories of today's woman—her troubles, her triumphs, her tears, her laughter.

And her ultimate commitment to love.

Four new titles each month—get 'em while they're hot. Available wherever paperbacks are sold.   Temp-1

You'll flip . . . your pages won't!
Read paperbacks *hands-free* with

Book Mate • I

The perfect "mate" for all your romance paperbacks

Traveling • Vacationing • At Work • In Bed • Studying • Cooking • Eating

Perfect size for all standard paperbacks, this wonderful invention makes reading a pure pleasure! Ingenious design holds paperback books OPEN and FLAT so even wind can't ruffle pages — leaves your hands free to do other things. Reinforced, wipe-clean vinyl-covered holder flexes to let you turn pages without undoing the strap . . . supports paperbacks so well, they have the strength of hardcovers!

Pages turn WITHOUT opening the strap

SEE-THROUGH STRAP

Reinforced back stays flat

Built in bookmark

BOOK MARK

BACK COVER HOLDING STRIP

10" x 7¼". opened
Snaps closed for easy carrying. too

Harlequin Presents®

Coming Next Month

Available in March wherever paperback books are sold, or through Harlequin Reader Service:

In the U.S.
P.O. Box 1397
Buffalo, N.Y.
14240-1397

In Canada
P.O. Box 603
Fort Erie, Ontario
L2A 5X3